# THE KINGDOM OF THE BULLS

# THE KINGDOM OF
# THE BULLS

*A Story of Ancient Britain and Crete*

by
PAUL CAPON

ILLUSTRATED BY LEWIS ZACKS

W · W · NORTON *&* COMPANY · INC · *New York*

Library of Congress Catalog Card No. 62-16391

PRINTED IN THE UNITED STATES OF AMERICA

# THE KINGDOM OF THE BULLS

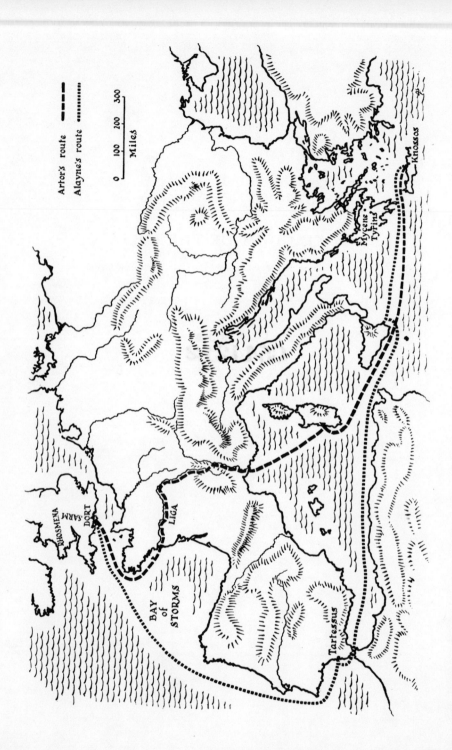

# Chapter One

THE younger Artor, son of Artor the Pendragon, was playing five-stones with several boys of his own age when a house-servant came to tell him that one of the peasants wanted to speak to him.

" Says his name's Badger-tail, my lord," added the servant, doubtfully. " He has an urgent message for you, so he says."

Artor was a little puzzled. " The only Badger-tail I know lives deep in the forest more than an hour from here," he remarked. " He's a woodcutter."

" So might this fellow be, my lord. He wears an axe at his belt."

" All right. Bring him to me."

The servant hesitated. " He says he must speak to you alone, my lord. And, apart from that, I doubt if I could get him into the house. He was almost too scared to knock on the door ! "

Artor laughed, threw the stones to the next player and stood up. Actually, he was quite glad of the interruption. He had only joined the game because the other players were guests and it was his duty to please them, but the game was rather a boring one. Anyway, it was difficult not to be bored on the day before the Feast of Yele, which always seemed as long as a year.

He remembered Badger-tail well. " I spent a night in his hovel once," he told the servant as they made their way to the main door. " That was the summer before last when a friend and I lost ourselves in the forest, then had the good fortune to come upon the woodcutter. My father rewarded him with a moleskin short-cloak."

" Ah — so he came by it honestly, my lord ? " murmured the servant. " I thought it looked a bit funny — a peasant wearing moleskin ! "

As he spoke the man opened the door and Artor found himself confronted by Badger-tail bowing so low that he nearly fell over.

He seemed dazed, blinking like an animal that is brought from darkness into bright light.

Artor dismissed the servant and led Badger-tail from the house. The evening was warm and humid. It had rained for most of the day, but now the sky was clearing and the weather looked as if it would be fine for the morrow's Feast.

" Well, what's the trouble, Badger-tail ? "

The old woodcutter, confused and tongue-tied, plucked his beard with one hand and beat the air with the other. " Your pardon, my lord . . . " he mumbled. " Wouldn't bother you, only . . . Well, he said it was urgent . . . Danger, he said — grave danger ! "

" Who said this ? "

" The foreign chap, my lord. Talked funny, like words were thistles in his mouth. Said he knew you."

" Did you get his name ? "

Badger-tail scratched his head. " Let me see . . . ' Oronees ' or something like that, my lord."

" Orontes ? " asked Artor, his interest quickening. " The trader ? I didn't know he was in Sarm."

" He said he mustn't visit the settlement. He's being watched or something, he said. That's why he sent me."

Suddenly, the old man opened his clenched fist and, lying on the grimy palm, Artor saw a small gold medallion in the shape of a fish, such as many of the traders wore round their necks as a protection against shipwreck.

" He gave me this, my lord, telling me to show it to you, so that you would know I spoke truth. Said I could keep it, if you so willed."

" I so will," said Artor, smiling. " But what about this message that you say is so urgent ? "

Badger-tail hardly heard him. He was gazing enraptured at the scrap of gold that had so unexpectedly become his property, making him the richest peasant in Sarm, and Artor had to speak sharply to recall his attention.

" Come, Badger-tail ! Give me the message quickly, or I'll have to take that golden fish away."

The woodcutter's hand closed abruptly over the medallion, and anxiety flickered in his eyes. " Your pardon, my lord . . . "

" Never mind about that. What had Orontes to tell you ? "

" He talked so funny it hardly made sense, my lord . . . Perhaps I didn't rightly understand him. I mean, what mortal would dare harm a high-born maiden such as the Lady Alayne ? "

" Alayne ? " echoed Artor, frowning. " You mean, my cousin ? "

Badger-tail nodded, shuffling his feet. " ' Grave danger ' were the words he used, and I was to go to the Pendragon and warn him. As if a peasant may speak to the Pendragon just when he pleases ! Besides, I told him, the Pendragon will be in council with his warriors, as is the custom on the eve of the Feast . . . ! "

Artor interrupted the muddle of words with a gesture and led the old man to a pile of logs that were waiting to be cut up for fuel. " Sit down, Badger-tail," he said, pointing to one of the logs, " and try to collect your thoughts. Let's begin at the beginning. Where were you when Orontes approached you ? "

" Outside my hut, my lord, making fire, and a hard job I was having for the tinder was damp and the flint hardly big enough to hold . . . "

" From which direction did he come ? "

" From the south, my lord, walking fast along the track the traders have used these last three summers. At first I thought he was a spirit, or perhaps a god, for he had enough gold about him to . . . "

" He was alone ? "

" Ay, my lord. Except for a white dog, and even the dog had gold in his collar. So he hails me, asking me if I'm a man of Sarm . . . "

" All right. Now tell me the message."

" My lord, he asks me if I know the Lady Alayne, daughter of the Pendragon of Dort, and I tell him I've never seen her, but that I've heard she is as beautiful as sunlight shining through the trees. He asks me if I know that she's in Sarm and I say I could have guessed it, for who isn't in Sarm on this midsummer of all midsummers ? He . . . "

." The message, man ! " put in Artor, losing all patience.
" What was it ? "

" Why, my lord, simply that the Lady Alayne is in grave
danger and that you would do well to stay by her side throughout
the Feast and until all the guests and strangers have departed. More
than that he would not say, but gave me the golden fish and asked me
to tell you that he would visit you as soon as possible to explain."

That was the whole message and Artor was inclined to agree
that it made little sense. After all, what possible ill could befall
Alayne at a time like this when every single one of Sarm's
warriors was practically within a stone's throw, to say nothing of
three hundred warriors from Dort and nearly twice that number
from Rhosmena ? So much for friends, but where might possible
enemies be lurking ? Amongst the contingent of half-savage
tribesmen from the east ? It was possible that some of them might
think to carry off Alayne and hold her to ransom, but it was
unlikely — for one thing they had too much respect for the might
of Sarm and, for another, the traders had little to do with them,
so how could Orontes have heard of their plans ? Then there
was a group of lordly warriors from the distant south-west, but
it was inconceivable that they should entertain criminal designs
and, besides, they were far too rich to be interested in holding
either Sarm or Dort up to ransom. That left only the traders
themselves, who were attending the Feast to the number of about
eighty, and Artor would never have dreamt of suspecting them
had the message come from anyone else than Orontes. As chief
shipmaster, he would know if they planned any mischief, but it
seemed ridiculous to suspect them of it. Presumably they wanted
to go on trading with these lands — they had an especial regard
for Sarm's fierce, brave bulls — and that they should care about
seizing Alayne for ransom was out of the question. Why, a single
one of the traders' ships would yield more gold, silver and
bronze than all Dort and Sarm put together !

Artor stood up. " Badger-tail, there's a mistake somewhere,"
he murmured, bringing out his elder-bough whistle. " You
must have misunderstood the trader. He speaks our language
but poorly."

" Very poorly, my lord," agreed Badger-tail, also rising.
" These foreigners are an ignorant crew, for all their gold and
linen. Why, I've a grandchild not yet four summers who can
speak words better than this Orontes ! "

Artor laughed, then warned the old man not to talk of the
message. " We don't want trouble arising from what is almost
certainly a misunderstanding," he said, " and, as for the Lady
Alayne, I can look after her. Yet you did right to come to me."

He blew a couple of notes on the elder whistle and, when the
servant appeared, told him to take Badger-tail to the back door
and give him food and drink, and also somewhere to sleep if he
wished to stay the night.

Artor wondered if he should say anything to his Aunt Morva,
who was Alayne's mother, but decided against it. To do so
would only make him look silly for taking seriously an almost
senseless message and callous for worrying his aunt unnecessarily.
After all, he was sixteen, he had been proclaimed a man just a
year ago, at the last Feast of Yele, and he wore a bronze dagger
to prove it.

Still, there would be no harm in having a talk with Alayne
and he went back into the house. Preparations for the Feast were
well under way. Stone cauldrons bubbled on the fires, servants
were skewering whole sides of beef on to the spits and the roof-
beams echoed with the pounding of pestles. The game of five-
stones had come to an end, and now most of the guests were
sitting around listening to a famous minstrel singing of wars
fought long ago. Amongst them was Alayne, and Artor could see
that she was a little bored. This wasn't surprising since the
minstrel sang in the Rhosmenan language, of which Alayne
couldn't understand a word, and she greeted Artor with a long-
suffering smile as he came and sat down at her side.

" How long does this saga go on for ? " she whispered.

Artor grinned and warned her that the minstrel was only just
getting into his stride. " He sings of the wars of seventeen kings,"
he told her, " and so far he has only reached the third. Fourteen
to go, and some reigned a very long time ! "

" Heavens, we'll be here all night ! "

" Then why not come for a walk ? The rain's stopped and everything's being made ready for the morrow."

" I daren't. Mother would kill me. She'd say I'd insulted the Rhosmenans by walking out on their saga. Could lead to a war ! "

Artor glanced towards his Aunt Morva, then smiled at Alayne. " She can't say much," he murmured. " She's fast asleep and likely to start snoring at any moment. Come on ! "

They waited until the minstrel was looking in the other direction, then crept away and slipped from the house.

The evening, as the sun sank towards the western horizon, was glorious and Sarm's great plain was flooded with golden light. Artor and Alayne strolled up to the high ground behind the settlement, whence they could look down upon the result of twenty years' labour — the great circle of standing stones, sixty in number, that had been wrested from the mountains of distant Rhosmena and brought to Sarm almost inch by inch. They had been trundled on rollers, dragged on sledges, floated on rafts and at times even carried bodily. Four like them had been lost on the sea-voyage, drowning eight sailors and two warriors, and yet another was on its way. This was said to be the greatest stone of all and it was expected at dawn the next morning, making the coming Feast of Yele memorable above all others.

Now the great stones bore garlands of wild flowers in honour of the Feast and within the circle sat the Council of Warriors, deliberating upon Sarm's policy for the year that lay ahead and presided over by Artor's father, the Pendragon. No boy could be prouder of his father than the younger Artor, for did not everyone speak of him as a great man and look upon him as the most able ruler this side of the water, even although he was still only in his thirties ? During the twenty-two years of his reign, he had made Sarm what it was — prosperous, respected and famous throughout the world for its Stone Circle, which had been his conception and his alone. He had built the Circle to glorify Yele, god of Sarm, and Yele had rewarded the land with peace, riches and freedom from pestilence.

All round the Circle, beyond its ditch and counterscarp, peasants were building up huge piles of brushwood and bracken that tomorrow evening would burn as bonfires, and at the entrance to the Circle, near the holy Yele Stone, they had erected a tall pole painted red and blue with ochre and woad. This was traditional and in a rougher age the maidens of the settlement had tried to climb it, believing that the first to reach the top would be the first to find a husband, but nowadays they contented themselves with holding hands and dancing round it, an activity that Artor and his friends thought rather silly.

Beyond the Circle were the camps of the visiting warriors, as well as a small group of tents housing the foreign traders. Those tents were easy to distinguish for they differed from the others in shape, colour and material. They were made of cloth rather than leather, the cloth was dyed crimson and the tent-poles were topped with golden trucks that caught the rays of the setting sun and gleamed like stars.

Strangely, it was Alayne who first mentioned the shipmaster.

" I wonder why Orontes hasn't turned up," she murmured.

Artor glanced at her keenly, but, as far as he could tell, her remark was no more than a casual one.

" Perhaps he didn't come with the traders this year," he suggested.

" Oh, but he did ! I saw him in Dort before I left."

" To speak to ? "

" Not really. My father invited him to a banquet together with the traders' captain and the deputy shipmaster, so I didn't really get a chance to talk to him." She was silent for a moment, then added : " The other two are here in Sarm. I met them strolling together this morning and asked them what they had done with Orontes, but they pretended they didn't understand."

" Pretended ? "

" Well, perhaps they really didn't understand, but I spoke very slowly, and surely they would have understood Orontes's name. Somehow I thought they seemed a little shifty. Guilty, even."

Artor pondered her remark and a possible explanation of Badgertail's confused message occurred to him. Perhaps Orontes had said something of this sort: " I want you to go to the settlement

and warn my friends, the Lady Alayne and the Lord Artor, that
I'm in grave danger. I may want their help and tell them I will
get to them as soon as possible to explain."

Badger-tail could easily interpret such a message, as spoken by
a foreigner, to mean that Alayne was in danger, and Artor
wouldn't be at all surprised to hear that Orontes had quarrelled
with his captain. There had never been any love lost between
them and the only reason the captain went on employing the
shipmaster year after year was that he couldn't do without him.
No one knew the local coasts as he knew them and he had a gift
for handling ships and crews that few could equal. On the other
hand, the deputy shipmaster was a nasty piece of work. His
name was Sarpedon, he was a toady and a braggart, and quite
cunning enough to have persuaded the captain to put him in
charge of the trading fleet. So, if the two of them planned to
murder Orontes, where better to do it than in a place as remote
from their native land as Sarm or Dort ?

" What are you thinking about, Artor ? " asked Alayne, as
they started to stroll down the slope.

" The traders and their ways. Some day I'm going to visit
their land."

" But you couldn't live there, Artor ! The heat is too great.
Their sun is much bigger than ours and from dawn to dusk the
sky is a blazing mass of flame. No one not born under that
terrible sun can survive it for more than a day."

" I don't believe it. That's no more than a tale put about by
the traders to keep us away. It is true that their summers are
warmer than ours and their winters milder, but they have the
same sun as we have."

" Who says so ? "

" Merwun the Sage."

" But he's in his dotage, Artor ! He's seen ninety summers if
he's seen one, and the years have left him with no more wits
than a new-born babe ! "

" I think you're wrong, cousin. I think he's still the wisest man
in Sarm, my father not excepted."

" But he's not ! He's a dear old man, but he's a dotard. He's so addle-pated he no longer believes the evidence of his own eyes."

" What do you mean ? "

" Why, last summer, when he visited Dort, he told me that he'd decided that the world was not flat ! Just because when a ship sails towards us we see first its mast, then its sails and finally the hull, he had come to the conclusion that the world might be curved in all directions like the top of a mushroom. He didn't seem to realise that if it were all the sea would run away ! "

Artor laughed and remarked that he knew that the sage sometimes had wild ideas, but that didn't mean he was senile. " Anyway, I believe him when he says that any of us could live in the traders' land," he added. " After all, he was born in those parts."

" Yes, almost a hundred years ago. He's forgotten what it was like, and some of the things he says about those lands are as silly as dreams. Once he even told me that they have animals as big as bulls, yet as tame as dogs, on which men can sit and be carried about from place to place."

" Well, a bull might be trained to carry a man on its back."

" Not any bull that I've seen ! And then he said that they have things for which we have no name, but which are like ships that travel on land and they do so by means of round pieces of wood fixed to their sides ! But that's nothing, because, according to him, the people in those parts can make their words and thoughts endure for ever ! "

" Did he say how ? "

" Not really. I just let him meander on, but I remember something about little squares of soft clay or wax, and the words or thoughts are made to appear in the wax as markings. Then they stay there for ever and anyone who sees the wax can understand what was said or thought even hundreds of years later ! "

" It certainly sounds a little far-fetched," agreed Artor. " Yet, you know, there might be something in it. I mean, think of the imprint of an animal's foot in mud. When we see such a footprint we know that an animal has passed that way even though it may have been days before. We can tell which way it went, what sort of animal it was and whether it was running or walking — "

" That's different altogether ! " exclaimed Alayne, interrupting him. " An animal's a thing, but a word is only a noise. Noises can't make marks in mud or clay or wax or anything else ! "

Artor nodded glumly, and reflected how odd it was that Alayne, although a girl and two or three months his junior, often had a quicker grasp of essentials than he had. Also he was a little disappointed. Momentarily he had had a vision of a world in which men could send long messages to each other even although they were hundreds of leagues apart and without having to rely on a messenger's memory, and in which all the history, learning and poetry of a people could be baked into clay and handed down from generation to generation.

They were nearing the Circle. The Warriors' Council was about to adjourn and Artor could hear the Circle's servitors intoning prayers to Yele. Between the garlanded stones he caught glimpses of the warriors, impressive figures in their ankle-length moleskin rain-cloaks, and felt comforted. Surely no harm could befall the Pendragon's niece with such warriors, and so many of them, to protect her ?

The guardians of the Circle saluted them as they passed its entrance and Artor, in turn, saluted the Yele Stone with three fingers to his brow. From the Rhosmenan camp came the sound of choral singing, while some of the warriors from Dort were engaging the eastern tribesmen in an archery tournament. As usual the traders kept themselves more or less to themselves and several of them were playing a game of quoits. Their quoits were made of bronze and to Artor it seemed incredible that men could be so rich as to use metal for their toys.

The largest, most opulent tent was that of the traders' captain. He was a swarthy, black-bearded man, almost a giant, and, since the tent's flaps were open, Alayne and Artor caught sight of him as they passed. He was lounging on a heap of coloured rugs, drinking from a slender silver goblet and talking to Sarpedon, the deputy shipmaster. The cousins attracted his attention momentarily and, pausing in his conversation, he waved to them. Artor returned the salute and wondered if he was right in thinking that the captain had looked at them in a strange, mocking way. Or had his curious, appraising glance been meant merely for Alayne?

Artor couldn't be sure, yet in that moment he suddenly saw Alayne as other men must see her — not as a spirited, argumentative, wilful cousin, but as a singularly beautiful girl with waist-length hair the colour of sea-sand and eyes as blue as the morning sky.

# Chapter Two

ARTOR was up and dressed before dawn the next morning. So was the entire household and, as its members struggled into their clothes in the darkness, they made no more noise than ghosts. In particular, no one spoke and that was the tradition. Ideally, the first sound to be heard in the land of Sarm on the Feast day was the roar of the bull's horn proclaiming the sunrise. In ages past, barking dogs had been sacrificed to Yele for profaning the dawn of the Feast and even, it was said, wailing infants, but the present age was an enlightened one, the inflexible law had softened to become no more than a reverent custom, and an accidental cough or sneeze would hardly be remarked, let alone visited by death.

Still, it was a custom that even the birds observed, Artor reflected, as he stepped out into the cool air of early morning, for not a bird sang and the world was so silent that he could hear cattle moving across the plain half a mile away. A shrouded moon lent a little light to the scene, just enough for him to see that a procession was already forming in front of the house. He joined it, slipping into his appointed place immediately ahead of the three senior remembrancers and immediately behind his two uncles by marriage, King Pansedo of Rhosmena, and Trist, the Pendragon of Dort, who was Alayne's father. Farther behind would come the senior household servants, together with their wives, for this was the one day in the year when women could enter the Circle without desecrating it.

Alayne and her mother emerged from the house and both wore new flowing dresses of the finest linen. Alayne's was pale in colour. There was not enough light for Artor to be sure of its actual shade, but he guessed it was green and, as his cousin took her place at his side, he gave her a " nip for new," something he had picked up from the Rhosmenans. Unluckily, it seemed that

Alayne was not familiar with the custom, for she gave a squeak of surprise and threw Artor a glance that was both angry and resentful. Her mother turned upon her frowning and so the day got off to a bad start. In fact, from that moment on there was an estrangement between the cousins that was to have serious consequences for them both.

Last to come from the house were Artor's father and mother — that is to say, the Pendragon Artor, son of Tola, and his lady, the Princess Robena, sister of King Pansedo. Attending them were the warriors that formed the household guard and also Pahto, the chief herald, who carried before him the great sword, Atoyele, symbol of Sarm's power, and now borne point downward as a sign that the land was at peace.

Out of consideration for Alayne's father, the procession moved forward very slowly, for the Pendragon of Dort was so crippled by rheumatism that he could only hobble along, supported on one side by his wife and on the other by a stick. He was a respected figure in Sarm, since years before he had brought the warriors warning of a foreign invasion, thus preventing them being taken by surprise and slaughtered to a man. On that occasion he had crawled, wounded in the knee, all the way from Dort and it was believed that the hardship he had suffered then was largely to blame for his present affliction.

No greater crowd had ever assembled within the Circle than gathered there that morning and, as dawn approached, every face turned to the east to gaze reverently at the Stone of Yele standing by the entrance to the Circle. Soon, if the count of days had been rightly kept, the sun would rise directly above the Stone and then the people of Sarm would be able to tell how they stood in Yele's favour. If the sun rose clear and golden, it meant that their god was pleased with them and would reward them with a year of prosperity, whereas the sun rising in redness and confusion meant that they had earned his anger and might expect some degree of punishment. The worst sign of all was a clouded dawn. It heralded famine, pestilence or invasion, and never once in the reign of the present Pendragon had the dawn of the longest day been anything but clear and bright.

Artor waited, standing beneath one of the three great trilithons — the arches formed by two standing stones with a third stone resting on them — and gazed towards the Yele Stone until his eyes ached. The sky grew brighter, the birds started to sing, and then Artor became aware that something was exciting the people at his back, those who stood on the ramparts of the Circle. He risked a quick glance over his shoulder. The men on the ramparts were nudging one another and pointing towards the west, but Artor saw no more because he suddenly became aware that his father was looking at him in stern disapproval, and he dutifully returned his gaze to the Stone just as the first gleam of daylight etched the horizon. At a signal from the Chief Servitor, the herald put the bull's horn to his lips and on it blew four great blasts of sound to proclaim the dawn of a new year.

As the last note of the fanfare died, a thunderous cheer went up from all assembled there and then everyone started talking at once. A little time would have to pass before the nature of the dawn became manifest, and meanwhile custom permitted people to relax a little and talk amongst themselves.

Artor glanced at his cousin. " Alayne, what are the men on the ramparts looking at ? "

She gazed at him coldly, and shrugged. " How should I know ? " she muttered, and looked away.

" What's wrong, Alayne ? . . . Surely you're not upset merely because I pinched you ? "

The girl refused to reply and when Artor tried to explain that he had simply been observing a custom, she turned away, pretending a sudden interest in something her mother was saying.

Artor gave up and gazed bleakly at the group of servitors in the centre of the Circle as they consulted among themselves about interpreting the dawn. As far as Artor could see it was neither a really good dawn nor a really bad one. There was a certain amount of mist and redness, but the rim of the sun's disc was clearly discernible and, except for a single ridge of dark cloud, the eastern horizon was exceptionally clear. No doubt the servitors would put an ominous interpretation upon that one black cloud, but Artor was not particularly worried. He believed in Yele as firmly as anyone in Sarm, but he did not believe everything the servitors said about the god — that the sun was his right eye, for instance, and the moon, his left, and that he made his moods and wishes known to man by means of cloud-formations and star-positions. Artor had lived in Dort and Rhosmena as well as in Sarm, and he knew that the people of other lands had other beliefs. They couldn't all be right.

Nevertheless, when the Chief Servitor climbed on to the stone slab at the Circle's centre to make his prognostication, Artor listened attentively. The old man wasn't easy to follow. For one thing, he had lost most of his teeth and, for another, the interpretation was couched in an archaic form of the language, but it seemed that the unsettled dawn was to be interpreted, not as a sign of serious displeasure on Yele's part, but as a reminder to people not to forget their duty to their god. " He threatens no failure of the crops and no extreme disasters of any kind in the coming year," boomed the servitor, " but we are not to forget that catastrophe is his to command. We must serve him better ! We must be more generous in our gifts ! He has brought great prosperity to Sarm and we repay his generosity by becoming ever and ever meaner in our offerings ! The lambing season is well advanced, yet how many lambs have been offered up to the glory of Yele ? Not one ! How many kids ? Not one ! In the course of the last moon, nothing has been offered up except a few bushels of millet, some dried goat's flesh and a few dozen river-fish ! People of Sarm, what sort of provision is this for a great god ? "

There was a lot more in the same vein, and it was difficult for Artor not to smile, since he knew that all food given to Yele was, in fact, eaten by the servitors, with the result that they were by far the fattest men in Sarm. The month before the Feast of Yele was always a lean one for them, since food was being saved up for the great day, but no doubt they would do all right once the feasting started and they certainly took no harm during all the rest of the year. So Artor's attention wandered away, not to be recalled until he suddenly realised that the Chief Servitor was talking about the black cloud and addressing himself directly to the Pendragon.

" My Lord Pendragon, the cloud has much the same shape as the great sword, Atoyele," roared the old man, " and this alone is enough to connect it with our ruling house ! My lord, beware ! You yourself, or your consort, or someone of your kin, is in jeopardy ! Beware of false friends and look askance at some of those from distant parts who come bearing rich gifts . . . "

An uneasy hubbub drowned the rest of his words. As was the custom, all the leading visitors would be making the Pendragon costly gifts and the servitor's words embarrassed everyone. Sarm's warriors started shouting at the old man and Artor saw his father consult hastily with his mother, and then rise, holding up a hand for silence.

" My lords, silence ! " he shouted, then turned to the old man standing on the Slab. " Great and holy servitor, it is right that you should tell Sarm what concerns Sarm, but that which concerns me alone should be told to me alone . . . "

The ancient servitor looked confused, like one whose good intentions have been misunderstood, shouting broke out again and, before the old man could make any reply, his fellow-servitors had dragged him from the Slab.

The Pendragon spoke again : " My lords and honoured guests, great news has just come to my ears ! The work of twenty years nears its end ! I have just been told the last and greatest of the stones destined for Sarm's sacred Circle has arrived . . . "

Artor heard no more, but found himself borne forward in the stampede for the Circle's gateway. Everyone wanted to be first to touch the new stone, for this was believed to bring good luck, and each of the sixty stones already in place had been similarly greeted.

Later, when Artor looked back upon the events of that long day, he was to blame all the excitement for his failure to behave as he should have behaved. No doubt, as soon as he heard the Chief Servitor's warning, he should have gone to his father and told him of Badger-tail's message, but too much seemed to be happening all the time. First, there was the headlong rush to greet the new stone and, although Artor did not go with it all the way, for he had no chance to be among the first to touch the stone, it involved him enough to take his mind off Alayne's problems, and then he fell in with a group of his friends, who told him that an ox was being roasted whole up by the Warriors' Hall.

He joined them. In fact, he believed himself to be starving for he had had nothing to eat that morning and the thought of a thick, smoking steak cut straight from the loin of the roasting beast was more than he could resist. The stone could wait — in any case, it was being dragged closer to the settlement all the time by hordes of sweating peasants — and, as for Alayne, no harm could befall her in broad daylight and with every warrior in Sarm within earshot.

Nevertheless, throughout that wild morning, his gaze sought her out continually, to assure himself that she was all right, and her pale green dress made her easy to distinguish wherever she was, whether dancing round the Yele pole, talking and laughing with her friends or helping to serve Dort's famous bullace-wine, of which more than a hundred skins had been brought to Sarm.

There had never been such a feast. Following custom, everyone of rank toured all the houses of the settlement, sampling the cooking, and long before noon Artor had eaten beef, mutton, venison, lamb, kid and wild pork, to say nothing of half a dozen different varieties of fowl. Whenever he found himself near the Circle he tried to get to his father, to speak to him about Badgertail's message, but the Pendragon was so surrounded by speechmakers and guests bearing gifts that he could never reach him.

Artor found all the warriors talking of the richness of the traders' gifts. It consisted of several articles, almost all of them bronze — a great helmet fringed with boars' tusks, an amazing shield tall enough to protect a man from head to foot, a sword longer than a man's arm, yet as light as an arrow, and a dagger with a coloured hilt in which precious stones blazed and flashed. Rather oddly, the traders presented the Pendragon of Dort with an almost similar set of gifts — oddly, because Dort's Pendragon was himself a guest and was anyway too crippled to make use of the weapons — and the jewellery in gold and silver that they gave to the Lady Morva was quite as splendid as that given to Artor's mother. All this caused a certain amount of murmuring amongst the warriors, but it wasn't until much later that anyone realised what it meant.

The arrival of the new stone at the Circle created another diversion and, as its two hundred attendant peasants hauled it up the last slope, Artor found its size and magnificence breath-taking. Up-ended, it would have been more than three times his height and, unlike the other stones which were bluish in colour, this one had a pale green hue and it sparkled in the sunlight as if it were encrusted with jewels. A stoneworker who had accompanied it on its journey told Artor that, again unlike the blue stones, it had not come from the mountains, but from a place near the sea-shore and that dressing it had been a slow and tedious business because of the stone's hardness.

Before the stone was formally handed over to the Circle's servitors, Merwun, the great sage, was brought to see it, for he had played a leading part in the making of the Circle and the placing of this last stone as its centre would crown his efforts. Too weak to walk the mile or so that separated his house from the Circle, the old man was borne thither on a litter and with him were his deformed servant, Gug, and his housekeeper, the widow Vivyan. Alayne had not exaggerated when she said that the old man had seen more than ninety summers and now he looked so frail and lay so still on the litter that it would have been easy to suppose he was on his way to his funeral.

Artor decided that the venerable sage was too old and feeble to understand what all the excitement was about, but he was wrong. No sooner had the litter been set down than the old man seemed to come to life and, helped by Gug, got shakily to his feet. His thin brown hands caressed the stone's rough surface lovingly, then his gaze fell on Artor and he beckoned to him.

" Artor, son of Artor ! " he cried, and for all its shrillness his voice was still impressive. " Come here and tell me your thoughts on this matter."

Artor approached him, grinning a little sheepishly, and the old man went on : " What does Sarm's Circle mean to you, young man ? "

It was a difficult question to answer, but Artor did his best. " I see it as a wonderful achievement, my Lord Merwun," he said, and he hoped he sounded convincing.

Merwun nodded two or three times, then said : " The Circle is Sarm's heart. It is more than a temple, more than a meeting-place, more than an instrument to tell the day of the year, more than one to tell the time of day, for, although it is all those things, it is first and foremost a monument to the spirit of the people who built it. Man is mortal, but mankind is immortal and may these stones stand for ever to remind all who see it that the power of men is without limit."

The old man turned from the Circle to Artor and, fixing him with a remorseless gaze, added : " More especially still, young Artor, it is a monument to the genius of your father, the Pendra-gon, whose conception it was and who carried the project through in the face of every sort of opposition, even to the point of threatening the Rhosmenans with war to make them keep their promise to supply the stones. Artor, do you realise that when he first conceived the idea of a stone circle he was younger than you are now by at least a year ? "

" Yes, my Lord Merwun," whispered Artor uneasily, and was relieved when the old man suddenly lost interest in him and turned to the stoneworker to ask him some questions regarding the dressing of the stone.

It was all very well for old Merwun to talk, but Artor knew that his father's boyhood had been spent in more stirring times than the present. His opportunity had come when Sarm suffered invasion, but how could a youth make his mark when peace reigned in all quarters and when Sarm was too strong for anyone to dare to make war on her ?

Occupied with these thoughts, Artor happened to catch sight of Alayne strolling with two of the younger traders. She was trying to teach them the language of Dort, all three were laugh-ing, and Artor suddenly felt guilty when he remembered that he still had not spoken to his father of Badger-tail's message. Now it was too late, for the Pendragon was engaged upon the famous " tour of Sarm ". This was the most important ceremony of the

Feast, but, since its rites were secret, Artor knew little about it except that its purpose was to ensure a bountiful harvest and that, in the course of it, all the principal crops were visited by the Pendragon and his consort. They were attended only by the Chief Servitor and the Chief Remembrancer, and it would be late evening before the quartet got back to the settlement. As Artor saw it, the only other possibility was to speak to Alayne's father and mother, but this he was reluctant to do. Alayne's parents were extremely devoted and, if they thought for a moment that danger threatened their daughter, they would be quite capable of putting her under a heavy guard, even of locking her in the house. If that happened Alayne, in her present mood, might very well suspect him of inventing the story out of spite and then she would never forgive him.

Anyway he felt he ought to make one more effort to speak to Alayne herself and, to that end, he set out upon an elaborate manoeuvre that presently brought him face to face with her as if by accident. She was still with the young traders, and her smile faded as soon as she saw Artor.

He tried to make his greeting sound cheerful, but perhaps he overdid it. " Why, hullo, Alayne ! How goes it ? "

" Thank you, Artor. I'm enjoying myself."

" Good," said Artor lamely, then, since the others were about to pass on, realised he must take the bull by the horns.

" Alayne, may I have a word with you ? "

" Of course. What is it ? "

The two young traders were smiling quizzically, making Artor feel awkward and uncouth, but he was determined to stand his ground. If he failed to give Alayne some sort of warning he would never forgive himself, so he said, firmly : " I mean, alone."

Alayne frowned faintly, but Artor's tone must have impressed her, for, with a murmur of apology to the traders, she came to him and let him take her aside.

" Alayne, you remember we spoke of Orontes last night ? "

" Yes."

" I pretended I didn't know he had come with the fleet this year, but actually I'd had a message from him. Concerning you."

At last she looked interested and, as briefly as he could, he told her of the message Badger-tail had brought him.

She gazed at him as if she only half-believed him, then asked why he hadn't told her of the message the night before.

" I didn't want to frighten you."

" And now you don't mind ? "

" It's not that. It's just that seeing you with these fellows — "

" Artor ! " she snapped, flushing angrily. " You're not to speak of my friends like that. These ' fellows ' as you call them are men of breeding. One of them's the son of the traders' captain, and neither is so boorish as to pinch a girl when she's least expecting it ! "

" I'm sorry about that, but I thought you understood. Anyway, this other thing is serious. You don't think I'm making it up, do you ? "

" I don't know, Artor, but I'm certain I'm not in any danger from the traders — "

" The message didn't say you were."

" No, but you implied it, and I don't like it. Why, some of these men I've known since I was a little girl and I'm sure I can trust the two I'm with to take care of me ! "

Abruptly, she flung away from him and returned to her friends. Artor heaved a sigh, reflecting that girls were impossible, but at the same time seeing Alayne's point of view. After all, who would dare to offend the Pendragon of Dort by offering injury to his daughter ? No one, and especially not the traders, whose livelihood depended upon maintaining good relations in all the lands they dealt with.

# Chapter Three

A DEEP booming sound shook the air and momentarily Artor thought it was thunder until he realised that it was the peasants making their noisy music. This provided the traditional climax to the Feast, as from all over Sarm the peasants advanced towards the Circle beating their drums, warbling on elder-branch flutes and trumpeting on rams' horns. The rhythm was age-old and traditional. It went: *Ta-pom-pom-pom ; ta-pom-pom-pom ; tum-tum-tiddle-tiddle-pom-pom-pom !* and it was a rhythm that would be beaten out faster and faster as the night wore on, until by moon-rise the Circle itself would seem to be dancing to its frenzy. As well as playing the peasants feasted, and it was the one night in the year when any peasant might eat as gluttonously and drink as copiously as the greediest warrior in Sarm.

Artor met two friends of his heading for the house. " Time to paint, Artor ! " shouted one. " Come on ! "

Artor joined them and, putting his anxieties behind him, matched their high spirits with his own as the three of them raced, whooping and yelling, towards the house.

All the males in Sarm, except the very old and the very staid, painted or masked themselves for the Feast's evening festivities. Some disguised themselves as animals — as foxes, wolves or bears — or as birds, such as swans and eagles, while others used woad, ochre and chalk to turn themselves into the most fearsome-looking devils imaginable, and there were always several skeletons about — men who blackened their bodies from head to foot with soot, then chalked in the bones with startling accuracy. This year Artor had decided to disguise himself as fire and, to that end, he painted flames all over himself with red ochre and yellow clay picked out with smudges of burnt oak-bark to represent smoke. One of the women of the household had made him a head-dress from a goose's plumes dyed red and yellow, and by the time the disguise was complete the Pendragon himself would scarcely have recognised his son.

To preserve the peace during the night-time celebrations it was unlawful to carry weapons. The warriors had to bury their swords for the night or they might hand them for safe-keeping to aged relatives too infirm to join in the dancing and this was the course Artor adopted with his precious dagger. He handed it to his venerable Great-aunt Doda, but not without a pang at the

thought that this left him defenceless just when Alayne might be in danger. Still, the law was the law, to break it was to risk losing his ears and, apart from that, he would rather die than bring disgrace upon his father's house.

Artor caught another glimpse of Alayne as he returned to the Circle. She was dancing round the Yele pole with various girls of her own age. Presumably the traders had gone to their tents to put on their disguises. She saw him, but didn't recognise him, and in fact, called to her friends to admire his disguise.

" Who is it ? " asked one of the girls, as they crowded round Artor.

Breathless and laughing, Alayne tried to penetrate the disguise. " Why, it's Dokri, son of Pahto the herald," she cried. " Right ? "

" Wrong," said Artor, making his voice as deep as he could. " I am no man's son. I am Fire, Flame and Smoke . . . "

Alayne's smile faded. " Pooh, it's only young Artor ! " she exclaimed and ran back to the pole, followed by her giggling, screaming friends.

Artor was enjoying himself too much to feel upset. He knew his cousin very well. She could sulk with him quite effectively for a few hours, but he knew that by morning she would be her normal sunny and friendly self again. In any case, he had no time to think about his woes for just then the first of the peasants' bands arrived and a great shout went up to welcome the Lord High Misruler. This was a peasant, his identity unknown to all except a few intimates, who — in theory, anyway — would be master of all Sarm for that one night. His function was to direct the revels and, riding on the shoulders of his fellows, he was carried first to the Stone of Yele, which he saluted with three fingers to the brow of the huge, grinning mask that hid his face. He wore sheepskin robes and, as staff of office, flourished a rod to which were tied a dozen coloured bladders. Soon he would make a tour of the bonfires, to set them alight.

" Childish nonsense," remarked one of the lads with Artor. " If ever you become Pendragon, Artor, I trust you'll put an end to it."

" Not I," laughed Artor. " Being hit on the head with a bladder is a small price to pay for the peasants' loyalty. I've heard my father say that, but for the peasants, Sarm might still be under the heel of the invader. They fought like wolves ! "

" That I can believe, for they certainly eat like wolves. Come, let's have something more to eat before the bulk of them get here ! "

All round the Circle were fire-pits over which carcases were being roasted and to one of these Artor and his friends repaired.

Artor had the man-cook cut him a huge steak, then, clapping it between two halves of a barley-loaf, climbed up on to the counterscarp to eat it.

His friends joined him, each with food enough to last him for a week in leaner times, and from their vantage-point they could see people converging upon the Circle from all over Sarm. The noise was deafening. The earth shook with it and the pounding of the drums echoed and re-echoed among the great standing stones. Every single peasant seemed to have provided himself with a musical instrument of some sort, and the area round the Circle was so permeated with the music's rhythm that one felt that silence might never again return. Then, as the Lord High Misruler made his processional tour of the bonfires, leaping flames pierced the dusk at thirty or forty different points and from these fires sprang hundreds of smaller fires as the Misruler's followers lit torches in the blaze and waved them above their heads, until at last a great area of the plain was dotted with pin-points of flame dancing to the rhythm of the music.

The Circle itself was sacrosanct, but the revellers had no respect for its outworks and before long Artor and his companions had to jump down from the counterscarp as peasants by the score clambered up on to it and began racing crazily round and round the Circle with the flames from their torches streaming out into the twilight until it was as if the great stones formed the hub of a huge spinning wheel of fire, and sometimes a heavy splash was heard as a reveller slipped and fell into the muddy waters of the surrounding ditch.

Everybody danced. The music's hypnotic rhythm seemed to get into your blood and before you knew where you were you found yourself one of a long line of men and girls that surged back and forth in the gathering darkness and tried to force its way through similar lines of dancers. Shouts and screams rent the night continuously and sometimes the dancers made so much noise that even the music was drowned.

Among the wildest of the merrymakers were the traders and the disguises they wore were elaborate and costly. Bronze and silver ornaments flashed and jingled as they danced and many, with an extravagance that Artor could only marvel at, had decked themselves out in flowing robes of fine linen. Others wore masks representing bulls' heads, complete with enormous spreading horns, so that they were even a little terrifying, and it was the sight of a group of these fantastics that suddenly reminded Artor that he had seen nothing of Alayne for a long time.

He broke away from the line of dancers and thrust through the milling crowds until he gained the high ground beyond the Circle. He thought it would give him a vantage-point from which he would be able to pick out Alayne's pale green dress, but, as his gaze scanned the throng, he discovered that half the women in Sarm were wearing pale dresses and by now the light was too poor to tell their colours. Besides, the scene was veiled by clouds of smoke billowing from the bonfires and the evening grew darker with every minute.

As he stood there, wondering what to do, he heard a great bellow of laughter and turned to see the veteran warrior, Gar, son of Enga, strolling towards him with his lady on his arm.

" Young man, that's a fine get-up you're wearing," roared Gar. " What are you meant to be ? "

Artor told him and the old warrior congratulated him on the conception. " I musn't ask you who you are," he bellowed, " but you have the voice of Artor, the Pendragon's son."

" Good guess, my lord," said Artor, and for a moment he considered taking the veteran into his confidence.

The trouble with Gar was his impetuosity. If he thought any kin of the Pendragon's was in danger, there was no telling what action he might not take. For all his sixty years, he would be quite capable of plunging into the crowd and breaking half a dozen of the traders' heads as a first step towards getting at the truth.

So Artor checked himself and asked the old couple if they had seen anything of his cousin. " Her mother charged me to keep an eye on her," he said, " and I'm afraid I've lost sight of her."

" Your cousin ? " roared Gar. " The Lady Morva's girl ? No, no, I wouldn't recognise her — all these chits of girls look alike to me ! "

" Don't be silly, Gar," said his wife. " You mean Alayne, don't you, Artor ? The girl with the lovely fair hair ? "

" Yes."

The old lady glanced at her husband. " My dear, she was one of the girls playing tag over by Ullit's Copse."

Artor's heart missed a beat. Ullit's Copse was quite a long way away. He couldn't imagine what had induced Alayne to go so far from the safety of the Circle.

" When was this, my lady ? "

" Oh, I don't know. We've been strolling quite slowly and — "

" Just about sunset," put in Gar. .

" You say she was with other girls ? "

" Yes, several," said Gar's wife. " And several young men. Some of them were foreigners, judging by their wonderful disguises."

Artor thanked them and set off as fast as he could go. He skirted the crowds milling round the Circle and he was glad of the light given off by the bonfires, for now it was nearly dark and the moon would not rise for another hour. As he plunged down Sarm hill he came upon three or four girls making their way up it arm in arm with a number of young men. He recognised the voice of one of the girls and, calling to her by name, asked her if she had seen anything of Alayne.

" Yes, she's somewhere down by the Copse," came the answer, and suddenly Artor realised he'd been mad to doubt Orontes's warning. The shipmaster had known that a plot against Alayne had been arranged to coincide with the festivities and now it wasn't difficult to see how it had been carried out. Certain of the traders had decoyed her and various of her friends away from the Circle, and then they had separated her from her friends. But why ? Why should Alayne — " a chit of a girl " as Gar had called her — be so important to them ?

He ran on, came to the Copse and stopped for a moment to listen. The noise of the Feast still filled the night, but from near at hand came other sounds — the rustle of men moving through the undergrowth and words muttered in a foreign language. Then he heard Alayne. She was laughing, but he could tell she was near to tears and he could hear her pleading with her tormentors. " You are beasts ! " she cried. " Let me get by — *please* ! . . . I'll get into a terrible row from my mother."

Artor flung himself into the Copse and almost at once nearly tripped over something leaning against a tree. It was a broken axe-helve and he grabbed hold of it gratefully. There was still enough left of it to make a serviceable club, and so lucky was he to find it that he felt Yele must have guided his steps. He heard Alayne's voice again and now she sounded almost hysterical. " Listen, beasts ! " he heard her cry, " I've got a brooch-pin in my hand and, if you don't let me get past, I'll jab you ! I mean it ! " She was panting heavily, as if she'd been running about for a long time.

Closer to Artor, a man laughed and, guided by the sound, he moved in that direction. He came to a clearing and there was still just enough light for him to make out the figures of five or six men. All had their backs to him and they stood about in lounging attitudes, gazing at a point on the clearing's far side. Peering in that direction, Artor could just make out the skirt of Alayne's dress. She was lurking behind an oak and he guessed that the foreigners were daring one another to go and get her. He almost hoped one would try it. Alayne, in a bad temper and armed with a bronze brooch-pin, would be as formidable as a she-wolf.

One of the foreigners took a few steps towards her, holding out his hands peaceably. " Lady Alayne ! " he shouted, speaking the language of Sarm laboriously. " The game is over ! You win. Now we take you back to your people ? "

Alayne did not answer at once and Artor guessed that it was the warning he had given her earlier that made her so wary.

" Come on, Lady Alayne. We are all hungry. Let us take you to the Circle."

" You promise ? " asked Alayne.

" Of course."

Alayne moved cautiously from behind the tree and at the same moment Artor strode out into the clearing.

" Don't, Alayne ! " he shouted. " Run for it ! Make for — " Before he could finish the sentence the men were upon him.

Swinging the axe-helve, he caught one a glancing blow upon the shoulder and another a resounding crack on the head. In spite of the confusion, he was aware that Alayne was running towards him, calling his name, and again he shouted to her to get away.

She seemed not to hear him and, as two of the foreigners bore him to the ground, he saw the others rush at Alayne and sweep her from her feet. One of them slung her over his shoulder with no more ceremony than if she'd been a week-old calf and Artor hit the ground with her screams ringing in his ears.

He fell heavily. All the breath was knocked from his body and he decided his best tactic would be to feign unconsciousness. He hoped his assailants would leave him if they thought he could give no further trouble, but his hope died abruptly as he heard a dagger rattle from its sheath, and his blood seemed to turn to ice.

He closed his eyes tighter and commended his soul to Yele, but the expected blow never came. The two men were arguing, even struggling, and he guessed that one had hold of the other's wrist and was trying to make him drop the dagger. The argument seemed to go on for a long time and all the while Alayne's screams grew fainter as she was borne farther and farther towards the south. Artor's heart was thumping like a drum, he hardly dared breathe lest the men should become aware of his anxiety, and yet there was a moment when he almost wished that they would kill him and put an end to the suspense.

Presumably they were under orders to avoid bloodshed and, in the end, it was the man who remembered his orders that prevailed. The other gave in with a bad grace, snapping his dagger back into its scabbard and kicking Artor heavily in the ribs.

Artor just managed to suppress a groan, then realised that the men were leaving him, hurrying away in the direction taken by Alayne's captors. He waited until he heard them reach the brushwood on the far side of the clearing, then opened his eyes and sat up, rapidly considering whether he should go to the settlement for help or whether to try to track the foreigners. He decided upon the latter course. To return to the settlement would only be a waste of time. With all the warriors out of their houses and mostly in disguise, help would be difficult to come by.

His nose was bleeding, he had twisted his ankle when he fell and his ribs ached where he had been kicked, but he hardly noticed any of this as he hurried from the Copse. He was too intent upon heading his quarries off. His one advantage over them was his knowledge of Sarm. He could find his way even in the dark and, in spite of the foreigners' start, he felt he had a good chance of getting to the forest before they reached it.

He was sure they would make for Dort by way of the forest trail. It was the only route the younger traders knew and the larger part of their fleet was anchored off the coast of Dort. By this time Artor did not doubt that his adversaries were the traders, although he had not had a clear sight of any of them in the Copse and could not honestly claim to be able to distinguish their language from that of, say, the strangers from the distant southwest. Still, the evidence was strong enough. After all, the warning had come from Orontes, himself a trader, and why had the young traders paid so much attention to Alayne earlier in the day?

Limping a little he made for the bridge that crossed the stream at the foot of Sarm hill and he had nearly reached it when he heard voices. He flung himself to the ground and gazed towards the bridge. It was too dark for him to see much, but a certain amount of scuffling seemed to be going on and he heard a man curse angrily and then a muffled cry that could only have emanated from Alayne. He could guess what·was happening. The men who had captured Alayne had paused by the bridge to allow their colleagues to catch them up and to bind and gag Alayne. Nothing except gagging could account for her silence and, without it, she would have screamed at the top of her voice all the way to Dort.

Artor had caught up with the traders sooner than he had dared hope, and his spirits lifted. His plan was to overtake them in the forest and make for Badger-tail's hovel. The old man was a recluse and it was most unlikely that he would be at the Circle. He might be old, but he was as tough as hickory and he had enough axes and bill-hooks to arm a small army. Besides, he had a wife who was almost as massive as Gar the warrior and, if the three of them set upon the traders by surprise, they would stand a very good chance of freeing Alayne and putting the foreigners to flight.

The bridge creaked faintly and Artor took it that his enemies were crossing it. In fact, he could just make out their figures as dark shapes against the night sky. Their leader was a tall, angular man who could well be the deputy shipmaster, and he was followed by Alayne with a man on either side of her. The set of her shoulders suggested that her arms were bound tightly at her back and Artor could guess that her guards each held an elbow. Immediately behind her were two more men, so that, all in all, she could hardly have been better guarded had she been the fiercest warrior in the land.

Artor decided not to cross the bridge. Its creaking might give him away. Instead, he crawled on his hands and knees to the stream and plunged into it. It was cold enough to make him gasp, but it refreshed him and took the pain from his ankle and ribs. He reached the far side feeling he could overcome a score of traders with no better weapon than the axe-helve, which he still grasped, then he grinned as he reflected that it was as well he couldn't see himself — the water had made a mess of his disguise and he reflected he must look as if he'd just been dragged from a dyeing vat.

He pressed on, and even had to slacken his pace a little for fear of getting too close to the traders. They weren't hurrying and probably that was Alayne's fault. Unless they carried her they could go no faster than she would consent to go, and Artor knew she could seem very feminine and helpless when it suited her. At other times, she could run quite as fast as a man, but the traders weren't to know that.

Ahead lay the forest, just discernible as a broad ridge a shade darker than the surrounding darkness. Owls hooted gloomily and at his back Artor could still hear the throbbing of the peasants' drums beating out their unvarying rhythm. In the east a smudge of paler sky showed that the moon was rising and before long it would shine free of the low clouds that shrouded the horizon. Perhaps that was what the foreigners were waiting for ; perhaps they were reluctant to face the forest at its darkest.

Artor decided to take a chance on getting to the woods ahead of the traders. He left the footpath and, moving as fast as his injured ankle would let him, set out on a wide detour over rough broken country. He crouched almost double as he ran, and reached the forest just as the moon broke through the clouds and bathed the scene in its cold, unearthly light. He was less than a furlong ahead of his enemies and, until he had increased his lead, he dodged from tree to tree, but kept as near as he dared to the regular trail, because the undergrowth was sparser there.

Even at night, he had no fear of the forest. He had hunted in it ever since he had been given his first bow at the age of six and no one knew this part of it better than him, except perhaps old Badger-tail. Animals rustled in the undergrowth, once he heard a wolf yelp, but the winter was long past and he knew that no wolf would attack a man unless it were starving.

When he could no longer hear the foreigners' voices, he made for the centre of the trail — it was about nine arrow-shafts in width — and broke into a limping run. Moonlight filtered down between the trees, growing steadily brighter, and he had no fear at all of missing the path that led to Badger-tail's hovel. A storm-riven oak-tree stood close by it and he came upon it after he had been in the forest rather less than an hour. By then he guessed he was more than a mile ahead of the foreigners, and everything depended upon the speed with which he could mobilise Badger-tail.

The woodcutter's hovel stood in a small clearing. It was an old-fashioned, circular dwelling and Artor was surprised not to be greeted by the barking of Badger-tail's dog. Usually, when a stranger approached, it set up enough noise to awaken the dead and it was the one denizen of the forest that Artor was a little afraid of — it was a shaggy, malevolent, pig-eyed creature that would tear the throat from wolf, bear or man if its master told it to.

The dog didn't bark because it wasn't there. Its kennel was

empty and, with a sinking heart, Artor realised that he misjudged the woodcutter — like everyone else in Sarm he was at the Feast and no doubt he had taken his wife and dog with him.

The door of the hovel opened when Artor put his weight to it, but there was no one sleeping on the heap of dried bracken that served as a bed, the fire had been damped down with turves and even the woodcutter's prized collection of axes was missing — presumably the old man had hidden them before he set out for the settlement. All that remained were two or three helves and a small fragment of a flint axe-head, which Artor put in his kilt-pouch — it would serve to cut Alayne's bonds, but that was about all.

The set-back was an appalling one, and Artor was left with but one course open to him — he would have to tackle the foreigners single-handed again, with no weapon but a helve, and with no more hope of success than the element of surprise could afford him. If he dropped on to the traders' leader from an over-hanging branch he might be able to induce the others to panic and run, for they were men of the sea and no lovers of forests, which they believed to be inhabited by all sorts of unimaginable ghosts.

He hurried from the hovel by a path which he knew joined the main trail at a point well to the south. Brambles whipped him across face, chest and legs as he ran, but he paid no attention and did not stop until, with a suddenness that stood his hair on end, a tremendous shout echoed through the forest. It was accompanied by the barking of a dog, followed by the clash of metal on metal, and then, amidst more shouting came the sound of feet thudding at speed over the turf as if their owners were pursued by devils.

As soon as Artor had recovered from his astonishment, he forgot his injured ankle and flung himself along the path faster than he had ever moved before, but he arrived at the trail too late to head the foreigners off. He could hear them pounding along to the south of him and he was just about to set off in pursuit when another sound reached his ears — a low, agonised groaning, such a noise as might be made by a soul in torment.

He gave up the idea of pursuit, and ran northward along the trail to discover the source of that blood-chilling sound, reflecting also that it was just possible that Alayne had escaped in the scuffle. Shafts of moonlight lit the trail, and before he had gone more than a couple of furlongs he glimpsed something white lying on the turf not an arrow-shot ahead. He slowed down, holding the axe-helve in front of him like a quarterstaff, and now, as well as the groaning he heard another sound — a fierce deep-throated snarling.

Owls beat the foliage above his head, hooting mournfully, and suddenly it was as if the friendly forest had turned into a haunt of lost spirits and even the air seemed to grow chill. Artor shivered, sweating coldly, yet continued to move forward in spite of all his instincts telling him to turn and run for it. He peered through the half-light until his eyes ached and at last the whitish patch resolved itself into a man-shaped form lying across the trail. At the man's side crouched a tense, snarling dog and in a flash Artor understood something of what had happened.

He recognised the white, wolf-like dog as belonging to Orontes and knew that the wounded man it guarded could only be its master. No doubt Orontes had been lurking on the trail ever since moonrise, anxious to learn whether or not his warning had taken effect, and when he found that his one-time shipmates had indeed captured Alayne he had attacked them. As a reward he had received a stab-wound in the back and now Artor was near enough to see the dark patch of blood staining his tunic and slowly spreading.

" Orontes ! It's Artor . . . "

The shipmaster gave no indication that he heard. His groans were growing faint and Artor could guess that unless his wound was treated at once, he was in a fair way to die, but there was the dog to contend with. It crouched there snarling, baring its teeth and bristling, and refused to let Artor get within four or five paces of its master. At that distance he couldn't even hope to stun it with the axe-helve.

Its name, he remembered, was Polyxo.

" Good dog, Polyxo . . . Good dog . . . Steady now . . . Good old Polyxo . . . Good dog ! "

The dog relaxed a little, looked less ready to spring and its snarling became less confident. Artor edged forward, an inch at a time, and continued to hold the axe-helve warily in front of him. All might have been well except that just then Orontes muttered something from the depths of his delirium — perhaps he dreamt of the fight and urged the dog to attack — for in a flash the dog sprang, hurling itself at Artor as if it had been shot from a bow.

Artor was almost as quick and just managed to thrust the helve between the dog's jaws as he and the animal went down together. He fell on his back, with the dog's forepaws on his shoulders, and instinct led him to lock his legs over the dog's back and hold it to him.

The dog fought to get the axe-helve out of its mouth, whilst Artor struggled with all his might to force the animal's head back against the pressure of his leg-lock and so break its back, but the brute might have been made of bronze for all the impression he could make on it. Its eyes blazed redly, its great yellow fangs were no more than inches from his face and it gnawed away at the axe-helve as if it were a bone. It was only a matter of time before the helve broke and if, before that happened, Artor couldn't kill the dog, the dog would certainly kill him.

The strange, immobile struggle seemed as if it would last for ever. The strain on Artor's muscles converted itself into agony and, although he was strong enough to hold the dog, he was not strong enough to overcome it. The axe-helve, under the strain of opposing forces, presently gave an ominous crack and for the second time that night Artor commended his soul to Yele.

He closed his eyes and, with the last of his strength, made one more enormous effort, trying to thrust the helve upward and draw his legs down. The blood sang in his ears and just as his consciousness started to ebb away from the sheer magnitude of his effort, the dog gave a yelp of terror and momentarily Artor thought he had attained his end.

Something had happened at any rate. The weight on his chest

seemed greater and he opened his eyes to find that there were now two dogs above him, and the second one — Badger-tail's shaggy brute — had his fangs buried in Polyxo's neck. Badger-tail was there, for Artor heard his croak : " Let him go, my lord ! " and Artor released his leg-hold just as the two animals were dragged from him by an unseen hand.

He sat up, dazed and breathless.

The white dog had met its match and now it cowered against the ground with the shaggy monster standing over it ready to tear it apart at a word from Badger-tail.

Artor looked towards Orontes and saw that Badger-tail's wife was stooping over him, probing the stab-wound and easing the blood-stained tunic from the shipmaster's back.

The old woodcutter helped Artor to his feet. " Lucky we left the Feast early, my lord," he said, " or you'd have made dog's meat as sure as Yele made Sarm ! "

" Now then, Badger-tail," muttered his wife. " Leave the young lord be and make yourself useful. You're a great one for bragging how you know every tree in the forest, so go find a wych-elm and bring me a slip of its bark."

As Badger-tail, grinning in the moonlight, went off in search of a wych-elm Artor joined the old woman at Orontes's side.

" Will he live ? " he asked.

" No, my lord. Not he. Nor you, nor I, nor Badger-tail, nor the Pendragon himself. We must all go home to Yele when he calls."

" I mean, will he live now ? "

" Why, yes, my lord. Now and thirty summers besides. He's not the dying kind ! "

# Chapter Four

ALAYNE was so stunned by her kidnapping that for the first part of the journey she hardly knew what was happening.

Her capture haunted her mind as a half-remembered nightmare. A harmless game had suddenly turned into violent lawlessness, friends had become enemies, Artor had tried to rescue her, but beyond that point she had no clear memory of events, nothing except a confusion of impressions. She remembered screaming as she was borne to the stream, she recalled the bite of the thongs as her arms were bound and she remembered feeling sick as a wad of wool was thrust into her mouth and tied into place with a strip of linen, but otherwise there was nothing except an endless journey through an endless forest. It was as if, in gagging her, her captors had also stifled the power of thought, and so numb were her emotions that she was not even able to feel resentment.

Then just as it seemed that nothing could break the monotony of the journey, Orontes pounced. He and his dog came bounding from the undergrowth like avenging demons, Orontes to attack her near-side guard and his dog to fly at the leader's throat and bear him to the ground. The shout of terror uttered by the man as he fell played some part in recalling Alayne to herself and she felt that his agonised screams for mercy as he fought the dog would echo through her mind for ever : " Orontes, call the brute off ! Let us parley ! . . . Call him off and you shall have our captive ! "

Orontes called the dog off. Her captors raised their hands to show they were not armed, then Orontes came to her, saying : " Come, my Lady Alayne ! You and I will go to Sarm and tell your uncle just what manner of guests he's been entertaining. Turn about, child, and let me cut your bonds . . . "

Before she had time to turn, the leader of her captors — whose life Orontes had just saved — struck. She witnessed the treachery in detail, but, gagged, couldn't warn Orontes. Besides, it happened so quickly. She didn't recognise the leader for Sarpedon, since he was disguised as some fiery, mythical bird, but she saw his hand dart into the feathers that covered his chest and reappear with a dagger that flashed for an instant in the moonlight before he brought it down with all his force, plunging it into Orontes's back, then leaping away with blood streaming from the blade down his arm and on to his feathers.

Orontes slumped to the ground, groaning, and Alayne's captors had to keep the dog at bay with their daggers. Then the largest of them hoisted her to his shoulders and all four men set off at a gallop, striving to put as much distance between them and their leader's treachery as they could. The dog's piteous howls, as he guarded his wounded master, followed them through the night and to Alayne it seemed that she had fallen into the clutches of creatures more like devils than human beings. Pain racked her tightly-bound arms, the thongs that held the gag in place cut into her flesh and when at last, breathless and dishevelled, she was lifted to the ground, she was not far from losing consciousness altogether.

She would have fallen had not one of the men caught her and helped her to a tree-stump. The gag was removed, her bonds were cut and, as she rubbed her aching wrists, she realised that they had arrived at a clearing where there were two or three tents and a camp-fire. Men, huddled in blankets, were sleeping round the fire and now they started up as the chief of Alayne's captors clapped his hands and shouted some orders. This was the man who had stabbed Orontes, he had lost most of his disguise during the headlong flight and now Alayne could recognise him as Sarpedon, the deputy shipmaster.

He knew, by her look of horror, that he had been recognised and after a moment's hesitation he came to her. He cringed a little, like a dog currying favour, and his eyes flickered shiftily under his heavy brows.

" I'm sorry, my lady," he muttered hoarsely. " You must know that this is none of my doing."

" None of your doing ? " echoed Alayne, astounded. " What do you mean ? "

" I mean I am only acting under orders."

" Whose orders ? "

" I must not say, my lady."

" Where are you taking me ? "

" Again, I must not say, but I may tell you that the worst of your journey is behind you. Now food and drink will be brought to you and for the rest of the way you will be borne in a litter, ungagged and unbound."

As he spoke, a servant approached bearing a trencher on which were slices of cold venison and other provisions, but Alayne shook her head. She wasn't hungry. She had eaten a lot during the Feast and, besides that, her jaws ached so much that the very thought of eating nauseated her.

Sarpedon looked concerned. " You must eat something, my lady," he said. " It will be many hours to your next meal."

" I am not hungry," said Alayne, " and, even if I were, I should hesitate to accept the food of traitors."

Sarpedon gave her a shamefaced glance, and dismissed the servant. Then he beckoned to another servant who stood nearby holding a large beaker of wine.

" At least you will drink, my lady ? "

This was harder to refuse. Alayne's throat was as dry as a kiln and she knew that sooner or later she would have to accept her captors' wine. So it might as well be sooner. Besides, a plan was beginning to form in her mind and she would need to keep up her strength if she were to carry it out. Almost certainly she was being taken to the coast and, to reach it, her captors would have to bear her through the heart of her own country. By then it would be daylight and, although the litter she rode in would undoubtedly be curtained, the sound of the breakers would tell her when the sea was near. There were fisherfolk all along the coast and, if she then started screaming and shouting, she thought she would stand some chance of being rescued by her father's subjects.

So she said : " Yes, I should like some wine," and accepted the beaker from the servant's hands.

She drank thirstily and had to admit to herself that the traders' wine was better even than Dort's bullace-wine. She had tasted it once before, as a guest of the traders' captain, and he had told her it was made from a fruit that did not exist in Dort. This fruit, he said, grew in great clusters on a vine and each of its berries yielded more juice than any five bullaces, but no doubt he exaggerated.

As she drained the beaker it suddenly came to her that she had made a terrible mistake in accepting the wine. Its dregs had a bitter taste and, with a sense of shock, she remembered a sage-woman telling her that there were certain herbs, such as henbane, that, bitter to the taste, had the power of sending a person to sleep against his will.

What a fool she had been not to suspect a trick ! Was it likely that her captors would carry her through Dort in broad daylight ungagged and unbound . . . and undrugged ?

Perhaps it was her imagination, but already drowsiness seemed to be creeping over her and she panicked, knowing that there would be no hope of rescue unless she could keep awake. She glanced about her wildly and saw that some of the servants were already preparing a litter such as the traders' captain habitually rode in. They worked by torchlight and the dancing flames were reflected brilliantly in the litter's cloth-of-gold hangings and showed that it was furnished sumptuously with soft, lamb's-wool cushions. It would be impossible to stay awake in such comfort and she hastily told Sarpedon not to bother about the litter.

" I'd sooner walk," she said, but Sarpedon did not reply and the last thing she remembered was his swarthy face smiling down at her sardonically. Behind him the trees swayed in the moonlight, and then the night itself seemed to rush upon her like a torrent of darkness . . .

It was full daylight when she at last awoke and her impression was that she had been asleep for an infinite length of time. At first she could form no idea of her whereabouts, her head ached violently and her skin grew clammy with horror as it came to her that the kidnapping, the stabbing of Orontes and the wild flight through the forest were not merely incidents in a nightmare, but things that had actually happened. Wherever she was, she was still a prisoner and still in danger.

She was lying amidst cushions in a deep hammock, walls of red canvas surrounded her, and momentarily she thought she must still be in the litter, but the swaying of the hammock was too rhythmic for that, and when she became aware of seagulls screaming and of the creaking of timber, the truth swept over her like a douche of ice-cold water.

She was on shipboard, and the ship was at sea !

She could hear the rattling of the great sweeping oars in their rowlocks and the monotonous chanting of the helmsman just above her head.

She pushed her disordered hair away from her face and struggled into a sitting position. She still wore the green dress that had been new only the day before, but now it was torn, soiled and crumpled, and she noticed that her wrists still bore the marks of the thongs that had bound them. Yet, apart from the brutality of her capture and the drugging, her captors had treated her well and also as if they still recognised her as a Pendragon's daughter. Since it was clear that she had not been taken as a slave — no potential slave would be carried in a litter or allowed a cushioned hammock to sleep upon — why, why, why had she been kidnapped ? It made no sense at all, and all the traders would gain from it would be the undying enmity of her father.

Her head swam as she climbed from the hammock and she had to steady herself by gripping its lashings. Her apartment was a tent of sorts and she guessed, from the nearness of the helmsman, that it was pitched towards the stern of the ship. The tent-flaps were laced together, but when she put an eye to a gap in the lacing she found herself looking straight towards the bows over the heads of the slaves who sat three to a bench as they groaned and strained over the great sweeps. The ship's great scarlet square-sail was furled to the cross-tree, since the ship was moving almost directly into the wind, and for the time being the sail was useless.

A dark-skinned youth dressed all in white squatted immediately in front of the tent and Alayne supposed he was her guard. He wore a curved dagger at his belt, but he seemed harmless enough with his slight figure and his shock of fuzzy hair and when Alayne started to unlace the tent-flaps he at once jumped to his feet and bowed deeply.

" I am hungry," she told him, and she thought he understood her for he smiled brilliantly, bowed again, then left her, swinging himself down a short ladder and disappearing beneath the half-deck on which her tent was pitched. However, he returned almost immediately and brought her, not food, but an ewer of water, a bronze basin such as would be worth a king's ransom in Dort, a towel of soft linen, a phial of cleansing oil, a comb and a mirror of polished silver.

Hungry though she was, she was glad to be able to wash and, as the youth placed the basin on the deck and filled it with water, she asked him his name. He grinned, not understanding at first, but when Alayne repeated her question with gestures she succeeded in conveying her meaning, for the young man pointed to himself and said, " Apulu ! " and also managed to indicate that he had been appointed her slave and bodyguard. This he did by scowling ferociously, drawing his dagger and slashing at imaginary enemies beyond the tent-flap, but Alayne guessed that the same dagger would be used against her should she attempt to escape by jumping overboard.

Once the idea of escape had entered her mind, it gave her no peace and, as she washed herself and combed her hair, she considered the possibilities. It was likely that the ship was still within sight of the shore and, if so, reaching it should not be beyond her powers as a swimmer, but there would be other things to contend with. The ship's archers, for instance, and, of course, as soon as she jumped the ship's boat would be manned and sent after her. Still, with the ship heading into the wind, its progress would naturally be slow and it was possible that her chance would come at night.

The wash freshened her, her head no longer ached and, as soon as her toilet was complete, she pushed aside the tent-flap and stepped out on to the half-deck. Apulu was nowhere to be seen, one or two of the slaves looked up from their oars and gazed at her with apathetic eyes, but their overseer was too busy to notice her as he marched up and down between the benches, swearing at his charges and slapping his armoured thigh with a rope's end.

Alayne glanced casually to starboard and momentarily felt sick with disappointment. The ship was out of sight of land ! Between her and the northern horizon there was nothing except an empty expanse of sparkling, sunlit sea with seagulls circling it ! Her heart sank and, at that moment, as a sense of the seriousness of her plight came to her, she almost gave way to terror. She was lost to Dort and it might well be that she would never see her native land again.

Apulu returned, bearing a great bowl of steaming food, and fortunately for Alayne her hunger proved stronger than her fears. Also she was fascinated by the idea of cooking on board ship and she wondered at the ingenuity of these foreigners that they dared to light fires when all about them lay timber, pitch and canvas, all things that would burn like brushwood if given half a chance.

The food was richer than Alayne was used to. It consisted of mussels cooked in barley with oil and strongly flavoured with saffron, and although she ate every crumb of it she wondered how long it would be before she again tasted the plain fare of her native Dort — the unseasoned beef, mutton and venison and the coarse barley-bread. Apulu also brought her a flagon of wine and, since her captors had nothing to gain by drugging her again, she did not hesitate to drink it.

Her breakfast over, she made herself comfortable in the hammock and pondered desperate measures. Apulu seemed a friendly, good-natured youth and she wondered if she could win him to her side. And, if him, why not the oarsmen ? There were nearly a hundred of them, all powerful men, and, as slaves, they must necessarily hate their masters. So what might they not do for the promise of freedom and a title to land in Dort ? Why, she could capture the ship and return to Dort in triumph ! Her mother, the Lady Morva, had been acclaimed as a heroine when she was a girl — she had carried a message by night through the great forests that lay between Sarm and Kedda — so why should not she, Alayne, emulate her, even surpass her ?

Unfortunately, there was the language difficulty. Apulu did not speak a word of her language, or she of his, and, as for the slaves, they probably did not even know that there was such a place as Dort, let alone that it had a language. They were never allowed ashore and in all things connected with their trade, the foreigners were amazingly secretive, fearful lest details of their routes and business-arrangements should be picked up by others. They were even secretive about the ships themselves, never anchoring close enough to the shore for their rigging to be noted and never allowing a fishing-boat to come within arrow-shot of them. All cargoes were rowed out to the ships in boats and when, as children, Artor and Alayne had implored Orontes to take them aboard one of the ships, he had assured them that it would be more than his life was worth.

The day grew hot and a new fear began to haunt Alayne's thoughts. How long would it be before they reached those latitudes where the sky was an unending mass of flame? Artor had said that there was no truth in those stories, but he didn't know, and she was much more inclined to believe the dictates of common sense. Why, everyone — except Artor — knew that if you sailed south it grew hotter and hotter until at last you came to the Land of Eternal Fire, whereas if you sailed north it grew colder and colder until eventually you found yourself in the Land of Eternal Ice. It stood to reason.

Before her fears had really taken hold, Apulu reappeared. He had a message for her and he did his best by mouthing his words and gesturing. Alayne caught the name " Sarpedon " and guessed that the shipmaster wanted to interview her, so, without hurrying, she swung herself from the hammock and spent some minutes tidying her hair and arranging her dress. Then she indicated to Apulu that she was ready and followed him out on to the half-deck.

Instinctively, she gazed towards the north, towards where she believed Dort to be, and caught sight of something that set her heart thumping as if it would break loose from its moorings. Hardly a mile from the ship were three fishing-boats casting their nets !

She realised that she must act at once, or she might never again get the chance, and, with thoughts of her mother's journey through the night-bound forest flooding her mind, she jerked her sleeve from Apulu's grasp and ran to the gunwale. She climbed on to it before anyone could stop her, hesitated for a split second — appalled by the distance between her and the waves — then jumped. Apulu's shout rang in her ears as she dived, only to be cut off as sharply as with a knife when she hit the water and went plummeting down into the sea's cold depths.

She was a quarter-furlong away from the ship before she surfaced and then, rolling on to her back for an instant, she caught a glimpse of the consternation her escape had caused. She could see Sarpedon on the poop, shouting orders, the great sweeps were at rest, sailors warped the ship's boat alongside and on the forecastle the archers drew their bows.

She took a deep breath and submerged again, swimming under water until she thought her lungs would burst, and when she next surfaced an arrow struck the water hardly an arm's length in front of her. She suspected it was aimed more to frighten than to wound, but for all that she quickened her stroke and swam like one possessed for the next two or three furlongs.

A quick glance over her shoulder showed her that the ship's boat was being manned, but she had a fair start and felt that she had a real chance of making good her escape if only the nearest fishing-boat would come to meet her. So far its crew had not seen her and although she wasted some breath in shouting to them she could not make them hear.

She asked herself if it would be possible for the boat to race the ship to Dort and safety. She thought so. The fishermen of Dort had taken to the new-fangled sail like ducks to water and already they were famous for their skill in handling it, whereas the foreigners still relied mainly upon their oarsmen. Fortunately, the wind, blowing strongly, was in the right quarter for a fast run to Dort, and the traders' ship had yet to turn and set sail.

One of the men in the nearest boat spotted her and pointed. His two mates joined him in the bows and all three gazed towards her, but showed no inclination to help. She shouted to them, but they stayed as still as statues and she fancied there was something

inimical in their attitude. She wasn't entirely surprised. The
fishermen believed it was bad luck for a woman to board a boat,
but no doubt they would think differently once they realised that
she was their Pendragon's daughter.

Once again she glanced over her shoulder and saw that the
ship's boat was about half-way between her and the ship, and its
oarsmen were rowing like heroes. She still had about a furlong to
swim, and she threw every ounce of her energy into the effort.
Never had she moved through water so fast, yet the fishermen, so
far from taking pity on her, started shouting angrily and shook
their fists. Momentarily, she trod water and cupped a hand round
her mouth. " I'm the Lady Alayne ! " she shouted. " Daughter of
Trist, the Pendragon."

The men behaved as if her words meant nothing to them, then
one of them spat over the side and another took up an oar and
started thrashing the water with it. He shouted something, but
his words made no sense to Alayne and suddenly the truth dawned
on her — these fishermen were foreigners and probably they came
from the land that lay across the sea from Dort, the land that,
some twenty years before, had sent an army of warriors into
Dort and Sarm to invade and conquer.

All hope of escape vanished and now there was nothing for her
to do except surrender meekly to the men in the ship's boat.
Nevertheless, even if Sarpedon punished her for her attempt to
get away, she was glad she had made it for anything less would
have been unworthy of the Pendragon's daughter. She turned and
swam slowly towards the ship's boat, and doing so noticed that
it was commanded by no less a person than Sarpedon himself. He
sat in the stern sheets and, so far from scowling, he was actually
smiling in her direction with something that looked like admiration.

The boat came about as she reached it and the helmsman, a
bearded giant, lifted her over the stern with hardly more trouble
than if she had been a drowning cat. One of Sarpedon's attendants
wrapped a blanket about her shoulders and handed her a towel,
and Sarpedon himself patted her cheek and told her she was a
brave girl.

" But then we always supposed you were," he added. " Otherwise, we shouldn't have chosen you."

Her teeth were chattering a little and she struggled to control them lest the foreigners should think she was shivering with fear. " What do you mean ? " she asked.

" No less than I say," Sarpedon told her. " You owe your present plight even more to your spirit than to your beauty."

" You talk in riddles," muttered Alayne, vigorously towelling her hair. " All I know is that you must be mad to make enemies of my father and uncle."

Sarpedon laughed, but did not answer at once since he was occupied with giving orders to the helmsman. Alayne looked towards the great ship, saw it as a symbol of the foreigners' immense power, and almost wished she had let herself drown while she had the chance. It was useless now to wish that she had paid more heed to Artor's warning and the thought that she would never see him again weighed more heavily on her spirits than anything else.

Still smiling, Sarpedon turned to her. " But we've not made enemies of your father or your uncle," he told her. " Why should they suspect us of kidnapping you ? There are many other strangers in Dort at this time."

" You're forgetting Orontes. He'll tell my father where the guilt lies."

" Orontes ? " echoed Sarpedon, flustered by this reminder of his treachery. " Orontes is dead. Have you forgotten ? "

" I know he was treacherously stabbed and I saw him fall, but I did not see him die. A groaning man is not a dead man."

" He's dead, I tell you," growled Sarpedon, scowling. " But, even if your father does suspect us, what can he do ? Has he a fleet other than a few score of fishing-boats, or an army other than a few hundred of quarrelsome warriors ? "

" He and my uncle can stop trading with you."

Sarpedon laughed again and asked her if she really thought that the ships made that long voyage merely for the sake of Dort's sheep or Sarm's cattle, fine though they were ? " No, child, what chiefly brings us to these parts is our ruler's need for tin, since without it we cannot make bronze," he told her. " There is no tin in Dort or Sarm, only in the south-western peninsula, and I've no doubt that the tribes in that area will go on supplying it as before. You may not believe me, but Dort is one of the least important places in the world ! "

It was pointless to argue and, as the boat drew alongside the ship, Alayne put the question that was foremost in her mind. " Where are you taking me ? " she asked, and this time Sarpedon answered her.

" You are on your way to the great city that men call Knossos," he told her, " but we shall take you no farther than Tartessus, since I have to return to Dort for the rest of the fleet. At Tartessus we shall transfer you to another ship, and then perhaps you'll learn why we seized you and what your future is to be, but of that I may say nothing."

Knossos . . . Tartessus . . . Alayne whispered the names to herself, but they evoked no image in her mind other than a pervading impression of terror and mystery, and she knew that not even the names would have been revealed to her had Sarpedon believed there was the slightest chance of her ever returning to Dort.

# Chapter Five

ORONTES did not die. He lost a lot of blood, his back was terribly gashed, but a rib had deflected the dagger from his heart and within three weeks of the attack in the forest he was well enough to be up and about.

By that time all Sarm's visitors had departed except for those from Dort. The traders' captain and his retinue also remained, but this was not from choice, but because the Pendragon had put them all under arrest as soon as he heard Artor's story. The captain swore he knew nothing about the kidnapping and accused Orontes of lying, and, when none of that availed, threatened Sarm with dire consequences unless he were set free.

The Pendragon, who had already had one experience of foreign invasion, realised that the threats were probably not empty ones, so he talked the matter over with Trist and together they decided they had better let the captain go. Consequently, he was put on board the smallest of the traders' ships with the warning never to show his face in either Dort or Sarm again, and permitted to set sail. He had no shipmaster to navigate for him, but the helmsman was a man of great experience and he was confident that he could get the ship at least as far as Tartessus. And so he might have done had not a terrible storm sprung up soon after the ship weighed anchor and had not the storm blown the vessel on to the great headland that marks Dort's western boundary. There it foundered with all hands and nothing was salvaged from it except a few bronze cooking-pots and a cask of wine.

Trist seized the three remaining ships in retribution for the loss of his daughter, and promised them as a reward to whomever could bring Alayne back. On that point, Orontes had something to say. Whilst lying in bed waiting for his wound to heal, a plan had formed in his mind and as soon as he was on his feet again he requested an audience of the two Pendragons. Also at the meeting were Merwun the Sage and young Artor. Merwun was there chiefly to act as interpreter, since Orontes did not speak the language of Sarm too well, and Artor was invited at the suggestion of his uncle, the Pendragon of Dort. The older Artor had objected to this, feeling that his son was too young to take part in the councils of men, but Trist had reminded him sternly that, in fact, young Artor was nearly two years older than the Pendragon himself had been when he rallied the warriors and threw the invader out of Sarm. " If we treat Artor as a man, he will behave as a man," he said, whereupon the Pendragon gave way.

The meeting took place in the Pendragon's house with rain lashing the thatch and a half-gale blowing. A small fire had been lit for the comfort of the aged Merwun, although it was mid-summer by the calendar, and all the household not concerned in the meeting huddled together at the far end of the hall, respectfully out of earshot. The Pendragon, who with the passing of the years had grown rather fond of the sound of his own voice, opened the meeting by speaking at some length. Since he told them nothing that they did not already know, young Artor's attention wandered until at last he heard his father say : " And so I call upon the foreigner, Orontes, to tell us his plan for the recovery of Alayne, daughter of Trist ; and in view of the wound already sustained by Orontes in her cause he will not be expected to stand while speaking."

Either the shipmaster did not quite understand the Pendragon or he refused to pay attention to a wound that he had been heard to describe as " a trifling scratch " — whichever it was, he rose to his feet, bowed ceremoniously to the two rulers and generally made it clear that he would not sit down again until he had said all he had to say. He had seen more than fifty summers, but he was still a magnificent-looking man, his curling hair was still as golden as it had ever been and his teeth as white. The sea, the wind and the sun had made leather of his skin, and there were few even of the warriors as well-muscled as Orontes — he was no swordsman or archer, but when it came to wrestling there wasn't a man in either Sarm or Dort he couldn't throw.

It was a strange thing, but the importance of the occasion seemed to give him an exceptional command of the language, he spoke it more correctly than Artor had ever heard him speak it and throughout his discourse he only had to appeal to Merwun for help on two occasions.

He said : " My lords, to make my plan clear, I must first speak of matters that may seem irrelevant to my purpose and I tell you this that you may not consider me merely a long-winded bore. As you know, it has never been the habit of us traders to speak of our travels except in the most general terms, believing that our livelihoods depended on keeping our routes a deep secret, even to the point of never mentioning cities and islands by their rightful names, but now all that, as far as I am concerned, has gone by the board for I am throwing in my lot with you.

" So let me tell you of two great and distant cities, Mycene and Knossos, that are like thunder and lightning to each other — linked by common origins, and yet essentially different. Knossos is the capital of a rugged and mountainous island, while Mycene is the chief city of a land as fair as Sarm. The two communities are for ever at each other's throats, sometimes one is in the ascendant, sometimes the other. Just now Knossos is the dominant power — and I have the misfortune to be a native of Mycene.

" Like myself, my father was a shipmaster — more than that, he owned a number of ships and it was he who first discovered the route to these lands — "

" I remember him," put in Trist, and Orontes nodded.

" No doubt you do, my lord," he said, " and I think you'll agree he was not a man to forget. Thirty years ago he and his associates had a monopoly of ' the northern trade ' as we call it, and they grew immensely rich selling tin to Knossos. Time and again the mariners of that city followed my father's fleet in an attempt to find out where the tin came from, but they were always outwitted and outmanoeuvred, and many's the ship they lost in the Bay of Storms or on the rocky coasts of the Western Isle.

" At last, fifteen years ago — open warfare flaring up between Mycene and Knossos — they resorted to piracy and lay in wait for my father's fleet as it returned home through certain straits that lie far to the south of here. Their ships outnumbered ours by three to one and they attacked at dusk, rowing down upon us with specially-wrought bronze rams fixed to their bows and with every ship crammed from stem to stern with archers. My father died with an arrow through his heart, two of our ships were sunk and those of us that survived the battle were taken into captivity.

" For some time before that I had been acting as my father's shipmaster and after the battle my captors tried to press me into their service, thinking to gain the northern trade, but there was no bribe gorgeous enough and no torture terrible enough to induce me to navigate their ships for them. I held out until the war came to an inconclusive end with a treaty that, on the face of it, made the two cities equal partners. Then, since it seemed that to serve Knossos was to serve Mycene, I overcame my scruples and agreed to introduce the ships of Knossos to the northern route. When presently I realised that we had been tricked and that the men of Knossos had no intention of honouring the treaty, it was too late to draw back, since by that time I had trained their best helmsman, Sarpedon, in the duties of deputy shipmaster, teaching him all the secrets of the route just as readily as my father had taught me."

At the mention of Sarpedon's name, Orontes's dog suddenly jumped up from the hearth and started howling, snuffing the air as if it expected to pick up Sarpedon's scent. It lay down reluctantly when Orontes commanded it to and for some time after continued to whimper and bare its fangs, so that Artor, remembering his struggle with the dog in the forest, hoped for Sarpedon's sake that the two never met again.

Orontes apologised for the interruption, then remarked that he had no more to say about past history.

" Now my concern is with the present," he said, " and for the first time in fifteen years I feel I stand within sight of revenging myself upon my enemies." He turned to Trist. " My lord, I'm

told that you have taken possession of the three ships that lay off
Dort and that you've promised them to whomsoever restores the
Lady Alayne to you ? "

" That is so," agreed Trist. " Though I have small hopes of
their ever being claimed."

Orontes was more optimistic. " I believe I can rescue your
daughter," he said, " but, since I certainly can't do so single-
handed, I shall be content with any one of the ships as my reward.
To help me I shall need warriors and artisans."

The two Pendragons exchanged glances and smiled faintly, then
Artor's father said : " Well, Orontes, we have warriors and to
spare, and we're always trying to keep them occupied in ways
that won't lead to trouble with our neighbours. But what manner
of artisans do you need ? "

" Such as were responsible for moving the great stones from
Rhosmena to Sarm," said Orontes. " So let me tell you what I
have in mind."

He told them he was sure that Alayne was being taken to
Knossos, and he explained that the island of which Knossos was
the capital lay towards the eastern end of a great inland sea.

" A sea that is entirely land-locked except at its western end,"
he said, " where are the straits I mentioned earlier. These straits,
less than three leagues wide and flanked by very rocky promon-
tories, are controlled by Knossos and it would be impossible for
us to enter the inland sea by that route — "

Trist frowned, interrupting him. " Yet you say there is no
other ? "

" None that has ever been used before," said Orontes, " but
I have some knowledge of a great river that flows into the Bay of
Storms. To reach its mouth you voyage westward from Dort for
some days, then you round a rugged and wind-swept peninsula
that forms the northern coast of the Bay of Storms. Presently you
come to the estuary of the river I speak of and, as a young man, I
spent a whole summer exploring it with my father. It is a
treacherous river, difficult to navigate, flooding readily during
wet weather, yet often too shallow for comfort during drought.
In spite of these hazards, my father and I explored it thoroughly

and discovered that it has its source far to the south. In fact, I am certain that its highest navigable point cannot lie so very far from the course of another great river that has its outlet in the inland sea."

His audience began to see what he was driving at, but he warned them hastily that, although the two rivers were separated by probably not more than fifteen leagues, a range of sizeable hills lay between. His plan was to take the three ships up the first river until they could go no farther, whereupon the ships would be beached and hauled westward overland until the second river was reached.

"We shall have a labour-force of more than two hundred rowers," he said, "and with the help of your artisans and by means of rollers and sledges it must be possible to get the ships over the hills even if progress is limited to no more than five arrows'-lengths a day. Should the natives prove troublesome there will be the warriors to keep them at bay, and other warriors can forage for food by hunting game and raiding granaries. Now none of this might serve any purpose were we eventually to reach the inland sea unsupported and at the mercy of any fleet Knossos might care to send against us, but it so happens that we shall not be without allies. '

"Allies?" echoed the older Artor, in surprise, and Orontes nodded. Some ten years previously, he said, certain noblemen of Mycene and allied cities had resolved not to live under the rule of Knossos any longer and they had fled westward by seizing two ships and manning them themselves.

"After many adventures," said Orontes, "they eventually managed to establish a colony on a small island that happens not to be so very far from the mouth of the second great river I spoke of. There they lead a hand-to-mouth existence, sustaining themselves by raids upon coastal settlements and other small piracies, but they are fierce, proud, resolute men and every one of them would gamble his life to strike a blow against Knossos. So, if our expedition joined hands with them, we should truly make a force to be reckoned with — a force that could boast five ships, a great number of seasoned warriors and a common cause. The power of

Knossos has grown weak through lack of opposition and a single blow struck resolutely at its heart might well topple it to the ground. And then, my Lord Trist, your daughter would be restored to you."

Trist looked only partly convinced, then asked Orontes if he knew why Alayne had been seized. Orontes indicated that he knew, but said that it involved matters of which he could not speak — deep and mysterious matters concerning which he was under a lifelong vow of secrecy. "But this I may say, my lord," he added. "Your daughter will never be treated with anything less than honour and respect."

"You can assure me she will come to no harm?"

"She will be accorded every honour," said Orontes, again, "and if any man offered her the slightest insult it would be more than his life was worth. More than that I cannot say."

It was not too satisfactory an answer, but Trist could see that he would get no other so did not pursue the matter.

"Well, my lords," said Orontes, moving towards the door, "that is my plan and no doubt you would like to talk it over in my absence."

He summoned his dog to his heels with a snap of the fingers and shouldered open the door against the hammering of the gale. Clouds of smoke belched from the fire, making the aged Merwun cough, and Trist turned to the older Artor.

"So, my Lord Artor," he said, "we are offered a desperate remedy for a desperate villainy, but, lacking any other plan, I have no choice but to fall in with it. But Alayne is not your daughter and I see no reason to involve you."

"Not my daughter, but my guest," said Artor, "and the crime was committed on the soil of Sarm. No, my Lord Trist, I stand with you in this matter and, as you know, I shall be only too happy to lend some of my more turbulent warriors to the cause."

Trist laughed, then they shook hands on it, although there was still the question of who should lead the expedition to be decided. No warrior of one land would agree to take orders from a warrior of another, and few warriors would agree to take orders from another warrior at all. Yet Trist, knotted by rheumatism, clearly could not take command, and they both realised that the older Artor could not leave Sarm. For twenty-two years he had kept the peace between the native warriors and the land-hungry men he had brought with him from Rhosmena, and he could continue to do so, but no one could tell what would happen if once he turned his back.

" What about Orontes ? " asked Artor. " You don't think he'd be acceptable as the leader ? "

" Not a chance of it," said Trist. " He is a trader, and my warriors have nothing but contempt for men who live by barter. No doubt they will accept his authority on matters pertaining to the ships and the sea, but that is all."

Deadlock had been reached, and a faint sound from old Merwun made the others look in his direction. So far, dozing with his head on his chest and with his hands thrust deep into his sleeves, he had hardly seemed aware of what was going on, but now his eyelids lifted and he was heard to mutter grumpily that time was when he had been consulted on matters of difficulty.

" Certainly, Merwun," agreed his Pendragon. " Why, have you a solution ? "

" Only the obvious one," said the old man. " You have a son who happens to be the cousin of the unfortunate young lady, who is the nephew of her mother, and who has reached years of discretion. I suggest that you invest him with your authority, place the ring of Sarm on his finger as a sign and let him lead the expedition."

The younger Artor was so startled by this suggestion that he could hardly believe his ears. Until that moment he had been hoping fervently that his father would allow him to go on the expedition, but that he should be its leader was beyond his wildest expectations. He glanced at his father's face to see how he was taking it and what he saw there was not encouraging. The Pendragon looked almost as startled as his son felt, and apparently he was not at all disposed to take the suggestion seriously.

However, Trist had no qualms about it and he put a gentle

hand on Merwun's shoulder. " Well said, Merwun," he murmured. " Of course young Artor must lead the expedition.
The warriors respect nothing except the ruling lineage and no
one can fault the boy on that score. What say you, my Lord
Artor ? "

Sarm's Pendragon gazed at his son uneasily and shook his head.
" But he's only a boy — " he began, only to be interrupted by
Trist.

" Were you more when we threw the invader from our lands ? "

" That was different. Authority was thrust upon me by my
grandfather's death and I had no choice but to accept it. I was
chosen for the task by circumstances more than anything
else."

Trist did not reply, feeling that since the reason for the expedition was so personal to himself he could not decently insist
upon Sarm's Pendragon sending his son with it, but Merwun was
freer to speak his mind and he proceeded to do so. He had no
awe of the Pendragon. He had known him since babyhood, had
acted as his tutor and had never hesitated to tell him when he
was about to make a mistake.

He said : " My Lord Pendragon, if you refuse to let young
Artor lead the expedition, you will be risking its success for no
good reason. Like most fathers, you see your son as younger than
he is and as less responsible. Certainly he is inexperienced
and largely untrained in the arts of war, but he is no fool
and he is well able to choose between alternatives and make
decisions. And that, for the most part, is what will be required
of him."

The older Artor waved a hand to indicate that he did not wish
to hear any more, then for some minutes he sat deep in thought
while the others waited in suspense wondering which way the die
would fall.

Then at last Sarm's Pendragon took the heavy, ancient ring of
Sarm from his finger and held it to his son to kiss. " Take it,
Artor, and put it on the first finger of your left hand," he said,
" and remember that once you are on board ship it will give you
as much authority over the expedition as I have over Sarm. From

then on you will speak, not for yourself, but for Sarm and its Pendragon."

Artor tried to control the trembling of his hand as he put the ring on his finger and he knew that if he lived to be a hundred he would never again experience quite the same sense of the miraculous as he experienced that day.

# Chapter Six

PRESENTLY the great white ship with the gilded bull's horns at its bows swung towards the east and Alayne guessed they were about to enter the inland sea that Sarpedon had spoken of before she was taken from his ship to this far more magnificent one. The cheerful, fuzzy-haired Apulu had been transferred at the same time and now he came to her and pointed to a towering rock that jutted from the sea about a league to the north. He tried to tell her something about it, but, although they had picked up some words of each other's language since leaving Dort, she could not entirely understand what he wanted to tell her. It was something about a famous being called Herakles, and she gathered that he was in some way responsible for the huge rock, together with another one that lay to the south. Shading her eyes, she tried to make out the second one, but the sun's glare, shining on the water, was too dazzling.

Now that she had got over her original terror, she was almost beginning to enjoy herself. Clearly her captors intended to treat her as a person of some importance, and the ship she was now on was an enormous improvement upon the traders' vessel, which, besides being old and battered, had reeked of pitch and bilge-water. The white ship was larger and more roomy, and its rowers, instead of being filthy and half-naked, all wore smart white tunics with pointed red-and-gold caps. In fact, it seemed unlikely that they were slaves, for they were not roped to their benches and no overseer paced up and down between their ranks flourishing a whip.

Yet, well treated though Alayne was, she realised that she was not the most important passenger on board. More important than her was a great white shaggy bull, one that was almost half as big again as any bull she had ever seen. He occupied a pen just aft of the rowing-benches and immediately for'ard of Alayne's own quarters, and he was secured to its rails by ropes as thick as a man's arm. Six grooms attended to his wants, washing and combing his rough coat three times a day, polishing his gilded horns, and changing his litter. For the most part the bull was strangely placid, but each morning, as the sun rose, he gave some indication of the power he could wield were he let free. Then, as daylight crept over the sea and the shadows shortened, he lifted his huge shaggy head and gave voice to a bellowing that seemed to fill the sky and, short-hitched though he was, the rolling and plunging of his great body rocked the ship so vigorously that the rowers could hardly use their oars. Full daylight seemed to pacify the beast and, as soon as the sun was above the horizon, he became calm again and would consent to eat the food brought by his grooms.

The bull's name, according to Apulu, was Leucoperses, which meant the " White Destroyer ", and he was of a breed of cattle, growing rare, called " aurochs ". What was more, he was the first white aurochs to be taken into captivity for over a hundred years.

Day after day the ship moved eastward over a smooth sea and beneath a burning sky, but Alayne was no longer worried about the heat. Apulu had managed to convince her that the sun was the same as the one that shone on Dort, and that the weather would never grow hot enough to kill her. She was ready to believe him, now that the ship no longer sailed south, but her faith was severely shaken when, a few days after entering the inland sea, she happened to look towards the north-east and saw, rising from the sea, a mountain with smoke pouring from its summit. This was on a day of appalling heat and, in panic, she looked from the burning mountain to the sea, wondering how long was left to her before the water started boiling.

Apulu came to her as soon as she blew the little bronze whistle he had given her for the purpose of summoning him, but when she pointed dramatically towards the mountain with its heavy pall of smoke, he dismayed her by smiling brilliantly and indicating that very soon the ship would turn in that direction. Then real terror seized her and she found herself wondering fearfully whether it would be better to die by burning with the ship or by scalding in a sea that had already taken on the hues of molten lead. Apulu saw what was in her mind and, taking her by the wrist, persuaded her to sit down and listen to him. He assured her there was nothing unusual about the mountain. It smoked like that all the time, and was never consumed. At night you could see flames coming from it, but it was only dangerous to those who lived immediately below it and the ship would not be going within a dozen leagues of it, to a place where it would put into harbour to take on fresh water and food.

Alayne felt comforted by his words, if not convinced, but for a long time after he had left her she continued to gaze towards the strange mountain. Still, it certainly did not seem to get any smaller, nor the smoke-cloud any larger, and after a while she decided that Apulu probably knew what he was talking about. By then, the ship had turned towards the north and was headed almost directly for the mountain, yet the heat was no greater than before and indeed the day grew cooler in the usual way as the afternoon wore on.

A rugged coastline crept into sight, and the early evening brought Alayne something fresh to think about. As usual her informant was Apulu. When he arrived with the fish and boiled barley that was her evening meal, he also brought a spare hammock which he proceeded to rig between two spars on the opposite side of Alayne's tent. "New stranger," he said and, little by little, Alayne learned that the ship was about to take on board another girl in the same plight as herself. Her name was Thara, her father was a petty chieftain ruling a small corner of the land they were coming to, and Apulu had been instructed to treat her with the same respect that he showed Alayne.

That was all he could tell her and Alayne could hardly contain her impatience as the ship struggled against the tide to round a headland and run into harbour. The idea of having a companion in adversity, an ally, someone she could talk things over with, was exciting and she prayed that the girl would be brought aboard before dark so that she could see what she was like. She wondered if she would be able to understand the language of Dort and decided that it was possible. After all, the people of Sarm understood it more or less, so there must be people of other lands that could.

The sun had set by the time the tide slackened enough to let the ship enter the harbour, but there was still sufficient light for Alayne to see something of her surroundings. The harbour was a natural one, quite small and rather disappointing after the splendour of Tartessus. The only vessels in it were a few shabby fishing-boats and the only buildings in sight were a dozen or so poverty-stricken hovels huddling between the harbour and the towering cliffs that enclosed it. No one seemed in a hurry to send the ship's boat ashore and as soon as the anchor was dropped the rowers stretched themselves out between the benches and shouted to the slaves to bring them their evening meal.

Apulu came to let down the sides of Alayne's tent and she asked him when the girl Thara would arrive.

" Not yet, not yet," he told her, when at last she got her meaning across. " In dark. You sleep, Lady Alayne."

She had no intention of taking his advice, but she couldn't help herself — the heat and excitement of the day had tired her and she fell asleep within minutes of Apulu lacing up the tent and leaving her.

She slept heavily and when at last she woke it was nearly full daylight and the ship was under way once more. A little time passed before she remembered anything about Thara, but as soon as it came back to her she sat up and gazed towards the other hammock.

It was occupied. Beneath its blanket was huddled a sleeping form, and a tangle of dark red hair covered the pillow. Alayne scrambled from her hammock and crossed the tent. Thara lay so still and breathed so heavily that Alayne guessed at once that she was drugged, just as she herself had been. Nevertheless, she whispered the girl's name a couple of times, then, getting no response, gently turned back the blanket from her face.

Thara was as beautiful as a goddess and, even with her eyes closed, her expression was imperious and unrelenting. In fact, there was something a little frightening about her and Alayne decided that she had never seen such strength of character in a face so young. Her shoulders were scratched and bruised, as if she had fought like a wild cat to escape capture, and when Alayne lifted the blanket she found that the girl was bound hand and foot. Her knee-length green tunic was torn in a dozen places, so that she might have been a beggar-maid but for the heavy gold bracelets she wore on both arms.

Alayne's impulse was to release Thara from her bonds, but second thoughts prevented her. If the girl chanced to wake up while the cords were being undone she might misunderstand the position and vent her anger on Alayne. The risk, Alayne felt, would be comparable to releasing a she-wolf from a trap.

Leucoperses, the bull, chose that moment to bellow his morning hymn to the sun and the ship's timbers shuddered as he struggled to his feet, stamping and plunging. Alayne hastily got into the splendid flounced dress her captors had given her and unlaced the tent-flap. She liked to keep an eye on Leucoperses during his morning exercise just in case he succeeded in breaking loose. He wore a head-halter, shoulder-harness and a double girth, and he was held by the ropes that secured him like a fly in a web, but for all that he succeeded in making the ropes and spars creak loudly as he heaved against them and when he raised his head and bellowed, he drowned even the noise of the waves slapping against the hull. It seemed impossible that anyone could sleep through such a din and Alayne glanced over her shoulder to see if Thara stirred.

The girl wasn't awake, but her breathing was lighter and once or twice her eyelids fluttered. Alayne had a jug of water by her hammock and now she took this and held it to Thara's lips. In a flash, the girl was wide awake. She jerked her mouth from the jug and gazed up at Alayne with such malevolence that Alayne might have been her deadliest enemy. Then, cat-like, Thara spat and before Alayne could stop herself she threw the water over the girl and backed away. She was relieved to hear Apulu's voice outside just then, asking if he might come in.

"Yes, come in, Apulu," said Alayne, shakily. "We're both awake."

Apulu had brought breakfast, two bowlfuls this morning instead of one. The food, a thick meat stew, looked slightly more inviting than usual, and Alayne remembered that the ship had taken on fresh supplies during its spell in harbour. She started eating, but kept her gaze on Thara, wondering what would happen when Apulu undid her bonds so that she could eat her breakfast.

However, he decided not to risk it. Instead, he approached her with the bowl of stew in one hand and a wooden spoon in the other, and made strange soothing noises as if he were attempting to feed a fractious child.

Thara glowered at him, waited until the bowl was only a few inches from her, then suddenly jerked upwards and knocked the bowl from Apulu's hand with her shoulder. The bowl smashed, most of the stew landed on Apulu's white clothes and, momentarily beside himself with fury, he whipped his dagger from his belt.

Alayne leapt at him, upsetting her own bowl of stew as she did so, and succeeded in dragging him away from Thara just as he was about to plunge the dagger into her back. Then his

senses returned to him and, rather sheepishly, he put the dagger
into its sheath.

The noise brought the deputy shipmaster running to the tent.
He was a dark, good-looking young man and, for some reason,
as soon as Thara saw him she became more like a wild animal
than ever, spitting, screaming and biting.

The young man quietened her by seizing a pillow from Alayne's
hammock and pressing it down upon Thara's face. She struggled
and kicked like a hamstrung mule, but he was too strong for her
and he managed to hold her down long enough to give Apulu
some orders. Naturally Alayne couldn't understand his words,
but she guessed that he told Apulu to clean up the mess and
fetch more breakfast for the captives. He also examined Thara's
bonds, as if making sure they weren't constricting the blood-flow
too severely, then gingerly took the pillow from her face. Her
shrieks were renewed and she kept the noise up until the deputy
shipmaster left the tent and was out of sight.

After that she fell silent, lying in her hammock and staring
sullenly into space. As Apulu tidied the tent and brailed its
sides, he explained to Alayne, more by gestures than words,
the reason for Thara's extreme hatred for the deputy shipmaster.
It seemed that he had engineered her capture. For months,
whenever the ship was in the little harbour, he had been paying
her court, pretending to be in love with her, and at last he had
succeeded in enticing her from the mountain fastness where
she lived with her ferocious father and brothers and go for
walks with him. She had had a tryst with him the night before
and he had kept it in company with a gang of kidnappers.

When Alayne heard that all her sympathy went out to Thara
and she decided she had been mistaken in thinking that her
captors weren't so dreadful after all. Yet she was puzzled,
and she told Apulu so. " But why ? " she asked. " Why capture
Thara ? Why capture me ? What does Knossos want with us ? "

Apulu looked startled and glanced involuntarily towards the
great bull, who, having made his protest, was now docilely eating
at his manger. " The bulls," mumbled Apulu, and with that
mysterious and menacing reply he hurried away.

The bulls ? Alayne looked at Leucoperses' massive flanks, at his powerful shoulders, at the incredible span of his horns and shuddered. She had heard of captives being set to fight wolves and bears, but never bulls ; anyway such things had happened only in the bad old days and surely nothing like it could take place now ? But why had Apulu been so evasive, just as if he'd been forbidden to tell her what the future held in store for her ? The subject of bulls seemed to embarrass him and she remembered that he had been equally vague when she asked him some questions about Leucoperses. She had wanted to know why such special care was lavished on the bull, why his horns were gilded and his coat washed, brushed and oiled and why he had six servants to look after him when she, a Pendragon's daughter, was allowed only one, but Apulu either couldn't or wouldn't tell her. On that occasion, too, he had vanished just as soon as he understood what she was asking . . .

Throughout the day Alayne made efforts to gain Thara's confidence, but it was hopeless. Thara ignored her and she also ignored Apulu. Whenever they tried to get her to eat or drink, she tried to bite their fingers or turned her head away, pressing her face into the pillow.

Apulu told Alayne that he wasn't too worried. He'd been in charge of other prisoners who had decided to starve themselves to death, but they had always given way on the second or third day, and Thara wouldn't be an exception. Alayne wasn't so sure. She doubted if Apulu had ever come across anyone with quite such a steely will as Thara, and she wasn't surprised when the girl spent the second day as she spent the first, lying in her hammock and either staring into space or gazing at Leucoperses.

The great bull seemed to fascinate her, as if she saw an affinity between his captivity and her own. Nothing else interested her in the least, not even the distant coastline that hung below the horizon throughout the day, nor yet a fleet of five trading vessels that passed within hailing distance of the white ship. She bore the heat stoically and even at noon, when it was as if invisible fire were pouring from the sky, she rejected all attempts to get her to drink and violently resented it when Alayne bathed her temples with a wet towel.

On the other hand, she no longer had the energy to be violent and when, late in the afternoon, the deputy shipmaster paid her a visit she merely glared at him balefully instead of screaming and kicking. He examined her bonds again, then spoke to her gently in her own tongue, telling her, Alayne guessed, that he'd remove the bonds if only she'd promise to behave herself. She had nothing to say to him and soon he left her, shrugging and heaving a sigh.

Perhaps Alayne imagined it, but during the day that followed she sensed a change in Thara. Two or three times she caught the girl looking at her, if not with friendliness, at least not with hatred, and now she made no objection when Alayne bathed her face and limbs with the towel. It may have been due only to exhaustion, but Alayne preferred to think that Thara's attitude towards her was softening and she was disappointed when she still refused to drink even so little as a mouthful of water.

Then, shortly before dawn the next morning, Thara's will-power failed her. Alayne first became aware of it when she was awakened by a strange, choking sound from the other hammock. She was out of bed and across the tent in an instant, taking the jug of water with her. There was just enough light for her to see that Thara was lying face downward sobbing and, curiously, her first reaction was one of impatience. She felt that the other girl, by this display of weakness, was letting her down. Then her better feelings came to the fore and, raising Thara a little, she held the jug to her lips.

Thara drank. She drank as Alayne had never seen anyone drink before, not pausing for breath until she had swallowed every drop, and then beseeching Alayne with her eyes for more.

Alayne put on her dress and blew her whistle to summon Apulu. He took his time about coming, so she opened the tent-flap and went out on deck. The ship was at anchor, snubbing gently at its cable, the rowers lay snoring between the benches, the great bull, his hooves tucked under him, dozed beneath a painted rug and the only sign of life was the sailor who paced the distant forecastle, keeping his watch.

Alayne blew the whistle again and at last Apulu came stumbling through the half-light, yawning and buckling on his belt. Alayne took him into the tent and managed to convey to him that Thara had surrendered, just as he had said she would. He nodded and produced the little knife he always carried on his hip. It had a blade of volcanic glass sharp enough to shave with and Alayne suspected that it was his most precious possession since he seemed to value it even more highly than his dagger.

He quickly cut the bonds from Thara's wrists and ankles, then picked up the jug and went to fetch more water and some food. Alayne took Thara's hands in her own and vigorously rubbed them to restore the circulation and as she did so she was momentarily surprised by the expression on Thara's face. She couldn't exactly describe it, but it was certainly not a defeated look. Rather, it suggested a mixture of triumph and cunning, as if a cherished plan were beginning to work out, and Alayne suddenly felt happier. She realised that Thara had not thrown up the sponge and, what was more, it seemed likely that she had decided she could trust Alayne. Otherwise, she would have taken care to conceal her feelings.

Apulu came back with some barley-bread, several smoked mutton chops and the water. He was looking pleased with himself and his attitude to Thara was faintly contemptuous. He represented the might of Knossos and now perhaps Thara would see how silly she had been to pit her strength against it . . .

That day Alayne's spirits rose higher than at any time since leaving Dort. She had found an ally, and one who was as gay as she was resourceful. Each had a lot of fun trying to teach the other her language and Alayne decided privately that Dort's tongue was much easier than the language spoken by Thara, in which the word for " hand " was quite different from the word for " hands", while the word for " water " was so long you could almost die of thirst in saying it. Still, they made a certain amount of progress, though, of course, not enough for Thara to be able to explain her plan to Alayne, and it wasn't until quite late that evening that it showed any signs of maturing.

As was Apulu's custom, he came to the tent soon after sunset to take away the used supper trenchers and to let down the sides of the tent. As soon as the tent-flaps were securely laced and Apulu had retreated, Thara touched Alayne's arm to attract her attention, then displayed a small object lying in her open palm. It was Apulu's precious knife, and Alayne was so astonished that she almost exclaimed aloud. Thara must have taken the knife from its sheath as Apulu stooped to pick up the trenchers, and Alayne's admiration for her was boundless.

" What are you going to do with it ? " she asked, but Thara, even if she understood, only smiled and looked mysterious, then hid the knife from sight.

At least Alayne had no worries on one score — Thara would not attempt suicide. She was far too resolute a person for that, but why did she want the knife ? Perhaps she had designs on the deputy shipmaster, but it seemed unlikely. The knife, with its short, deeply-convex blade backed with silver, was hardly a death-dealing weapon and, besides, how could Thara hope to gain the officers' quarters without being seen by the watch ?

Yet she would have to make use of the knife that night, or it would be too late. In the morning Apulu would report his loss, and then every inch of the tent would be searched until the knife was found.

Alayne knew she wasn't very good at keeping awake once darkness had fallen, but she was anxious not to miss anything and so for a long time she sat upright in her hammock with her arms clasped about her knees and her eyes wide open. She listened to the sounds of the ship heaving-to — the thumping of the oars as they were shipped, the splash of the anchor, the dull rumble of its cable as it ran out — and for long after, when the only sound was the lapping of the water against the side, she continued to stare into the darkness.

Yet Thara was sound asleep. Alayne could hear her deep, regular breathing, and presently she began to wonder if Thara had merely taken the knife out of devilment.

Suddenly she stiffened. As well as Thara's breathing, she could hear someone else's, and she had an idea that someone was fumbling with the lacing of the tent-flap.

" Who's there ? " she whispered.

She heard the would-be intruder catch his breath, then her fears faded as Apulu spoke, also whispering : " It's only me . . . Apulu . . . My knife . . . "

" Go away, Apulu. You mustn't come to the tent after dark. The shipmaster will dock your ears."

" It's lost ! . . . My knife with the silver handle ! . . . Please . . . "

" We haven't got it. Go away."

" Please, Lady Alayne . . . "

" You can look for it in the morning. Now go away, or I'll scream and wake the whole ship."

" No, no. Don't scream. I'll go . . . "

She heard the patter of his bare feet on the deck as he scurried away, but that was the last thing she remembered. Somehow or other, in spite of all her efforts to stay awake, sleep must have conquered her for when she next became aware of her surroundings it was darker than ever and she was lying uncomfortably in the hammock still clasping her knees.

She straightened herself and as she did so suddenly realised that she could no longer hear Thara breathing.

She was alone in the tent ! To make sure, she got out of bed and went to the other hammock. Except for blankets and pillows, it was empty.

A faint sound behind her almost stood her hair on end, then she realised that Thara was returning, creeping under the tent-flaps as silently and swiftly as a snake.

" Thara . . . "

" S-sh ! " hissed Thara, then put her arm about Alayne and urged her back to bed. She laughed under her breath, excited and triumphant, yet just what she had achieved was a mystery. Her action had certainly involved no disturbance, for silence hung over the ship like a blanket and now that the evening breeze had dropped there was not even the sound of waves against the hull.

After that, Alayne slept heavily and did not wake again until Apulu arrived with breakfast. He was rather earlier than usual, due no doubt to anxiety over his knife, and Alayne could detect impatience in his voice as he asked permission to enter the tent. She glanced at Thara questioningly, wondering what she had done with the knife, but Thara nodded, indicating that it was all right, and Alayne told Apulu to come in.

He found the knife almost at once. It was lying between the two hammocks partly hidden by a towel and he snatched it up with a wide grin of relief and implored Alayne not to tell the shipmaster. He would get into serious trouble, he said reasonably, if it were known that he dropped dangerous articles within reach of his prisoners.

He left them and‘ as Alayne started her breakfast, Thara shook her head at her and indicated that there was no time to be lost. Evidently something was about to happen and, following Thara's lead, she scrambled from her hammock and put on her dress.

Yet, when they went out on deck, everything was as usual. The rowers were either folding away their rugs or else sitting on the benches gnawing the huge hunks of barley-bread that served them for breakfast. Sailors stood by waiting to raise anchor at a signal from the shipmaster or his deputy, and the helmsman was lashing the great steering-oar into its lock. As yet the sun wasn't above the horizon, but Leucoperses was awake, lowing softly and snuffing at his litter.

Alayne glanced enquiringly at her companion, but Thara was gazing out to sea with an expression of extreme innocence, an expression that only relaxed for an instant as the great bull struggled to his knees and voiced a preliminary bellow. Then she became momentarily tense and glanced up at the shipmaster on the poop as if to make sure that he suspected nothing, and in the moment that followed confusion burst upon the ship with such suddenness that Alayne hardly knew what had happened, except that men were running in all directions and everyone seemed to be shouting at once.

The bull was loose ! As he rose to his feet to greet the sun, bellowing and swaying, rope after rope broke from him with no more trouble than if it had been cotton and then Alayne understood what Thara had been up to during the night — she had gone stealthily to Leucoperses and had severed each rope until it held by no more than a few strands. But why? What did she hope to gain by it?

Meanwhile, the confusion grew worse with every second. The bull, facing for'ard, was menacing the rowers, and they were trying to keep him at bay with their sweeps, each one of which was heavy enough to need three men to handle it. Already the ship was rocking violently, and the bull's grooms were helpless — Thara had had the sense to cut the ropes close to the harness and there was little to get hold of.

The bull had taken possession of the gangway between the rowing benches and, if a groom got near him, he had to do little more than twitch his huge flanks to send the man flying, and all the while those great sweeping horns flashed in the light of the rising sun. The oar-blades, striking the bull on his nose and chest, goaded him to an increasing fury, but did little to prevent his advance and soon the rowers were huddling round the mast's footing, a mob of terrified and desperate men. Farther they couldn't go, for at their backs, on the forecastle, were sailors armed with splicing spikes and grapples, who were only too glad to have the rowers between themselves and the bull. There were archers, too, and when one of the panic-stricken rowers leapt overboard he succumbed at once to a hail of arrows. The rowers might not be slaves, but clearly the archers had standing orders to shoot any that dived overboard.

Thara clutched Alayne's wrist, and Alayne had the impression that she was merely waiting for the confusion to reach its height before taking drastic action. But what sort of action? She had certainly caused a tremendous disturbance, but what could she hope to gain by it?

Still, she had no time to ponder the matter for suddenly the nature of the struggle changed dramatically. It came about when the rowers adopted new tactics, and made a barrier of their oars by turning them athwart the ship. Then, from behind this barrier, they were able to force the bull slowly back. Twice the great brute charged the barricade, then, baffled, he swung round and came plunging aft, towards the spot where Alayne and Thara stood. Ahead of him fled the grooms, fighting like madmen to avoid the dreadful, curving horns. One of them cannoned into Alayne, separating her from Thara, and, as she fell, she caught a glimpse of Thara streaking for the ship's side and diving overboard.

She was on her feet again in an instant, but it was too late. The bull had her cornered. Behind her was the break of the poop, cutting off her retreat, and in front was the bull, pawing the deck and preparing to charge. He was hardly an arrow's-length from her and she could actually feel his breath on her feet. She knew she had one chance of survival, and one only, and she tried to remember all she had witnessed in Dort when the herdsmen wrestled with the young bulls to capture them and bring them in to slaughter.

She knew that the bull would put his head down the moment before he charged and until that moment she must stay as still as a mouse. When he charged, he would be blind to everything else, but if she moved before he lowered his horns he would see the movement and gore her with a half-turn of his head. On the other hand, if she delayed her leap until he actually charged his impetus would carry him into the timbers at her back and she'd be crushed to death.

Days, years, centuries seemed to creep by and still the bull did not move. The gaze of every man in the ship was upon Alayne, yet none could help her. As long as the bull pawed the deck and stared full at her she was safe, but if anything distracted him and he turned his head the point of one horn or the other would catch and wound her, perhaps mortally. No one dared to move and nothing broke the silence except the creaking of the ship's timbers and the drip of water from its anchor-cable.

The bull snorted and its foot became still. Its great shoulders seemed to swell and then came the moment that Alayne awaited — the huge shaggy head moved down to present the horns, and she felt herself spring forward as if projected by a power outside herself.

She landed perfectly, dead between the bull's horns and with her arms about them. She locked her legs under the animal's jaws, and the bull, his eyes hidden by her clothes and body, stood stock still in terror, exactly as had the bulls of Dort. A cheer rang from end to end of the ship, the grooms raced forward and grabbed the bull by his horns and harness, and the deputy shipmaster himself lifted Alayne free.

She was a heroine to the entire crew. The sailors cheered her again and again as she was taken up to the poop to have her hand shaken by the shipmaster-in-chief, a venerable patriarch with a beard that reached to his waist. He patted her on the back, then a puzzled look crossed his face and he turned to his deputy. Alayne guessed that he was asking after Thara, and at that moment a shout went up and several of the sailors pointed out to sea.

Thara had escaped in the ship's boat. Already she was half a mile away, rowing clumsily but effectively and heading towards the north-west where a distant coastline was just discernible. Alayne's heart went out to her, yet she couldn't suppose that her friend had much chance of reaching land before the ship overtook her. Still, it was a brave attempt and she could only hope that Thara wouldn't be punished too severely.

She asked Apulu about it as he escorted her back to the tent. He grinned and said that Thara wouldn't be punished at all, for the simple reason that the ship wouldn't give chase. It was already a day overdue, and if Leucoperses was to arrive at Knossos in time for the Summer Festival, the rowers would anyway have to row throughout the last night at sea.

This meant little to Alayne, but at least it left her under no illusion as to how girls rated in comparison with bulls — a girl was only a girl, it seemed, but a white aurochs bull was almost a god !

# Chapter Seven

THE fog grew steadily denser, but Orontes had sworn not to give the order to heave-to as long as he could see the masts of the two vessels ahead. He was anxious to lose no time at all and, when the fog first closed in, he had explained to Artor that he could continue to steer a straight course provided he could see the masts of all three ships. " It's just a matter of holding them all in line," he told Artor, and at his side stood a seaman with a loud-hailer keeping in touch with the helmsmen on the other vessels and correcting any deviation.

The leadsman swung his line continuously, calling the depth of water after every cast, and the rowers' overseer had his men pause in their rowing after every hundredth stroke. The overseers in the other ships did the same, and then silence as heavy as the fog itself engulfed the ships. During the silence Orontes listened attentively for the sound of breakers betraying the presence of rocks or a foreshore and when he heard none he told the overseer to carry on, an order that was relayed from ship to ship.

One of the traders who spoke the language of Sarm told Artor that no other shipmaster would so much as move an oar in a fog this thick, but he said it with pride and Artor knew that Orontes had the confidence of everyone under him. All the shipmaster had to navigate by was a glaring circle of white light where the sun struggled to shine through the fog, but it enabled him to keep a southerly course and he told Artor he would hold that course until nightfall, when the three ships would anchor in the hope that the fog would lift during the night. For by then they should be nearing the point where they would have to alter course to the east, searching for the mouth of the great river that Orontes had spoken of, and they would need clear weather for the search.

The ships were overcrowded. Some of the traders, those who were old or had no stomach for a hazardous adventure, had been left behind in Sarm, but even so there was hardly room on board to turn round. For, as well as their usual complement of officers, sailors, archers and rowers, the ships carried between them more than a hundred warriors and about thirty artisans whose job it would be to engineer the hauling of the ships overland to the second of the great rivers. Room had been found for them in the forecastle, along with the sailors and archers, while the warriors, nearly forty to each ship, were packed like seeds in a pod into the space below the poop just aft of the rowers. Seasickness had subdued them for the first few days, but, now that the sea was as calm as a pond, they were growing restive and quarrelsome, and Artor had to be constantly on the alert for serious trouble breaking out amongst them.

The day dragged tediously, and Polyxo, Orontes's fierce white dog, was as bored as anyone on board. He spent most of the day lying crouched on the poop-deck with his head between his paws and his tongue hanging out, and Artor was the first to notice a sudden change come over the animal. Something seemed to disturb him all at once, making him prick his ears and shift his gaze from the rowers to the dense banks of fog beyond the ship's starboard quarter.

Artor drew Orontes's attention to the dog's uneasiness, but the shipmaster only shrugged. " His ears are sharp, my lord," he said. " No doubt he can hear porpoises playing out there, and hunting porpoises is a weakness of his. Perhaps you'd be so good as to hold his collar, or he'll be over the side in a trice."

Artor did as he was asked and in the same moment Polyxo sprang to his feet with his coat bristling and his lips lifting to bare his fangs. He growled softly and Artor reflected that if the dog really wanted to go overboard it would be a mistake to try to stop him. He had had a healthy respect for Polyxo ever since their fight in the forest.

The dog snuffed the air and began to bark. Then suddenly he

hurled himself so violently towards the companion-way that Artor had to let go of his collar to avoid being dragged down the steps. The warriors might have been a flock of sheep judging by the way Polyxo bounded over their recumbent forms and when he reached the gangway between the rowers' benches he raced along it as if he were coursing a hare. He gained the forecastle and stood there with his head over the starboard bow, while he made enough noise barking to drown the leadsman's chant.

Orontes was puzzled, and ordered a sailor noted for his sharp eyesight to join the look-out on watch at the masthead, but the man could see no more than his mate and for the first time Artor saw Orontes undecided. " What say you, my lord ? " asked the shipmaster. " We're making good progress, so are we to change course merely to satisfy a dog's curiosity ? "

" You don't still think it's a porpoise ? "

" No, because he'd've been in the sea by now. But I think it may be nothing more important than a fishing-boat or two."

" Nevertheless we'll investigate," said Artor, seizing the chance to assert his authority. " I can't think Polyxo would be so passionately moved by a fishing-boat."

Orontes nodded, and ordered the other ships to heave-to and stand off. Then, remarking to Artor that Polyxo's nose was as good as a star to steer by, he had the helmsman steer the ship a few points to starboard while the rowers on that side back-watered. Polyxo's bark dwindled to a sinister, blood-chilling growl and a few moments later the look-out shouted that he could see a vessel's mast and cross-tree above the fog.

" A cross-tree ? " muttered Orontes. " She's no fishing-boat, then."

" Could it be Sarpedon returning ? " asked Artor, excitedly.

Orontes doubted it, saying that even with the most favourable weather Sarpedon would not have had time to get to Knossos and back, but he ordered the archers to stand by with arrows on their bow-strings. The order excited the warriors and some would have drawn their swords had not Artor commanded them to hold. In their present mood, and as tightly packed as they were, it wouldn't have taken much of an accident with a sword to start them all fighting amongst themselves.

A momentary thinning of the fog gave everyone a glimpse of the other ship and a gasp of astonishment went up from the sailors as they recognised it.

" It's the *Paphos* all right," muttered Orontes, naming the ship that Sarpedon had taken, and it occurred to Artor that perhaps the vessel was still on its outward voyage. It was possible. It might have been damaged in the great storm of a few weeks back, and perhaps all this time it had been lying on a beach undergoing repairs. In which case Alayne would still be on board, and Artor didn't know whether to be glad or sorry. He was glad, of course, that Alayne might soon be rescued, but at the same time it was hard not to feel disappointed by the thought that the adventure might end before it had properly begun.

Someone aboard the *Paphos* was hailing them and one of the traders told Artor that Sarpedon was calling upon Orontes to heave-to unless he wanted to sail into a volley of arrows. Orontes ignored the threat and told some of the sailors to man the starboard bow with grappling-poles. Besides that, he ordered his other ships to row beyond the *Paphos* and cut off her line of retreat. Sarpedon must have heard the order as it was bawled through the loud-hailer and a moment later his voice was heard laughing raucously and hurling taunts at Orontes's head.

Orontes also laughed and told Artor that Sarpedon was accusing him of bluffing. " He says I've only got the one ship and warns me to surrender at once unless I want to end the day swinging from the cross-tree," said Orontes. " He says his crew outnumbers mine two to one, so I'm afraid he'll get a nasty surprise when he finds the *Paphos* boarded by trained warriors ! My lord, would you pick a dozen of your fiercest men to form a boarding-party ? "

Before Artor could reply the first flight of arrows from the *Paphos* screamed through the air and he saw one of the rowers slump over his oar with an arrow in his back. A sailor was also hit, but Artor had no time to take in anything more for he was too busy organising the boarding-party and stemming the clamour of those men not chosen.

It was the first time he had had to give the warriors any important orders and he felt that, on the whole, he acquitted himself well. Anyway, within a very few minutes of Orontes making the request, there were a dozen warriors manning the gunwales with drawn swords. Arrows whistled about their heads, but they stood there unflinchingly and virtually without protection for they had to hold on to the ratlines with their left hands and so could not raise their shields. One man was hit in the thigh by an arrow and Artor saw him pluck it out and throw it from him with no more fuss than if it had been a fly.

Orontes did not reply to the hail of arrows. Instead he told the archers to hold fast until the two ships met, and ordered the rowers' overseer to put on all possible speed. By now the *Paphos* was near enough for Artor to get some idea of the panic that reigned on board her. Sarpedon, over-confident, had not even troubled to raise anchor and now her sailors were hauling desperately on the cable in an attempt to render her free to manoeuvre, while the overseer's whip screamed amongst the rowers as they strained to get the *Paphos* bow-on to its enemy.

Artor expected Orontes to ram the *Paphos* amidships, or there-abouts, and he was surprised when, with the ships hardly fifty arrows'-lengths apart, the shipmaster had the starboard rowers ship their oars and in the next breath told the helmsman to use his steering-oar to back water. The orders seemed contradictory, but, as the ship slid towards the *Paphos* beam-on, it became clear that Orontes's idea was to do as little damage to the other ship as possible — after all, he intended to make her his prize — and Artor took his cue from this when one of the warriors not of the boarding-party asked him if he and the other fighting-men were to follow on as soon as the ship was boarded.

"No," said Artor. "Not unless I give the word."

This was badly received, but Artor knew the warriors. As

always, they were spoiling for a fight and they had only to get aboard the *Paphos* to start lopping off heads indiscriminately. There wouldn't be much point in Orontes taking care to preserve the other ship if he wasn't to be left enough men to run it.

However, there was one being on board who was not to be restrained, and this was the dog, Polyxo. He had been forgotten in all the excitement, but he was still snarling and growling on the forecastle and now, as grappling-poles were lowered and just before the two ships clashed, Artor saw him jump on to the *Paphos*, his white coat shining through the fog, and make straight for Sarpedon, bounding frantically over the backs of the rowers and tripping their overseer.

Sarpedon did not catch sight of the great dog until he was half-way up the steps to the poop and then the scream of terror that burst from his lips was cut short as Polyxo's fangs sank into his throat. No one had time to raise a hand in the man's defence before the impetus of the dog's frenzied rush carried them both over the stern into the sea, and that happened exactly in the instant that the two ships collided.

Artor was knocked to the deck by the impact, but he was on his feet again in time to see the boarding-party sweep on to the *Paphos* with swords flashing and flailing. The war-cries of Sarm, Dort and Rhosmena cleft the fog and Artor saw several of the enemy archers holding up the flighted ends of arrows as a sign that they would offer no resistance. Not that it availed them much, for the warriors were out for blood, and many a member of the *Paphos*'s crew hurled himself overboard in the belief that the sea would treat him more kindly than the warriors.

In fact, the fighting was all over in a matter of minutes. Apart from the archers, there were no trained fighting men on board the *Paphos* and, with their shipmaster drowned and with no cause to sustain them, the sailors mostly fell to their knees and begged for the mercy that the warriors were in no mood to show. Artor saw that he had to act fast if a massacre was to be avoided and, grabbing the loud-hailer from the helmsman's mate, he shouted to his men to stop the carnage and warned them, in the name of Yele, that he'd break the sword of any man who disobeyed. Only one man, a hot-blooded Rhosmenan, ignored the order — perhaps did not hear it — and he was in the act of running a sailor through when one of the other warriors knocked his sword up with his own. Artor caught a further glimpse of the Rhosmenan struggling in the arms of four or five warriors who were asking him, in tones of thunder, if he set the name of Yele, and Sarm's ring, at nought ?

Orontes beckoned to Artor. " Come, my lord," he said. " Let us board our prize and see what news we can gather of the Lady Alayne."

The crew of the *Paphos* cheered Orontes noisily as he stepped aboard, for he was popular throughout the trading-fleet, and soon he was surrounded by men swearing that they had only served under Sarpedon because they had been ordered to do so by the traders' captain. At least that's what Artor guessed they were saying, and he gathered that Orontes neither accepted nor rejected their pleas, but told them, first things first, that they had better haul their comrades from the sea, tend the wounded and swab the blood from the decks. He personally supervised Polyxo's rescue, for all this time the dog had been swimming alongside, barking ferociously.

The fog was clearing, condensing into heavy drops of rain, and as Orontes and Artor mounted to the poop, Artor caught sight of Sarpedon's body floating some way out, but easily recognisable by virtue of the brilliantly blue cloak worn only by shipmasters. Artor drew Orontes's attention to it, and Orontes told the rowers' overseer to have the body recovered and given a decent burial. " He was a good seaman whatever else he was," he remarked to Artor, " and besides, we don't want his spirit haunting these waters for all time, since they're quite hazardous enough as it is. So I've told the overseer to have the body sewn into sailcloth with enough ballast to sink it to the bottom ! "

The *Paphos* carried no deputy shipmaster, but the helmsman was an experienced and responsible man and Orontes questioned him regarding Alayne's fate. Artor could not understand the man's reply, which was a lengthy one, but he saw Orontes's face grow grave and the thought crossed his mind that perhaps his cousin had been overtaken by a calamity even more serious than kidnapping.

As soon as the helmsman stopped speaking, Orontes drew Artor aside and they sat down under an awning that graced the poop's weather side. It seemed that Orontes had asked the helmsman how it was that the *Paphos* had returned to these waters so soon, and the reason was that the ship had gone no farther than Tartessus. "There your cousin was put on board the White Ship," said Orontes, "and, although you will not understand the significance of that, I'm afraid it bodes ill for the Lady Alayne." He added, as if speaking to himself, "I had always supposed she had been kidnapped to serve as a hand-maiden in one of the temples of Knossos. With all respect to the Pendragon of Dort, it never occurred to me that she could be considered sufficiently well-born to interest the ministers of King Minos."

"King Minos!" exclaimed Artor. "I've heard Merwun the Sage speak of him, so he must be unbelievably old!"

Orontes smiled and shook his head. "No, no. He's not much over forty and in the prime of life, but the fact is that every king of Knossos is called ' Minos ' just as every ruler of another country bordering the Inland Sea is called ' Pharaoh ' . . ."

"Then what is Alayne's fate likely to be ?"

"My lord, as you know, I am under certain vows and cannot speak freely of the creed that is shared by Knossos and Mycene, but this I may tell you — that unless we can rescue the Lady Alayne before Knossos holds its Winter Festival almost certainly you will never again see her alive !"

Artor felt momentarily sick, then pulled himself together as he remembered that the winter was still many months away, but Orontes would not allow him even this small comfort.

"They call it the Winter Festival, my lord," he said, "but in fact it is held in the autumn as a preparation for the winter, and we have barely time for all the great tasks'that lie ahead !"

At least it seemed that for the time being the gods smiled

on them. A ship had been added to their fleet, the fog had given place to a moderate westerly breeze and long before nightfall the four ships were able to turn towards the east, heading for the mouth of the river that Orontes had explored as a young man.

# Chapter Eight

THE life Alayne led at Knossos was a strange, lonely and yet exciting one. For the first week or so she was so dazed by all she saw and experienced that she felt she must be living in some fantastic dream, and it was only little by little that she began to know homesickness and the terrible loneliness of not being able to speak to anyone, since no one spoke the language of Dort. Yet she was not alone, for she was one of six girls who shared a suite of rooms in a wing of the Great Palace. The other girls were all of her age within a year or two, all beautiful and, she gathered, all at least as well-born as herself ; and with one of them, Daphne, she struck up as much of a friendship as is possible between two people who cannot talk to each other.

Meanwhile, there was so much that was strange and marvellous. There was the city of Knossos itself and to Alayne, who had never seen collocations of human dwellings larger than the settlements of Dort and Sarm, whose only experience of stone buildings had been the one-storey houses of Rhosmena, 'Knossos, with its paved streets, towering buildings, painted walls, sweeping staircases and elaborate drainage system was a miracle of human ingenuity. She remembered how sceptical she had been when Artor had spoken of land-ships that went from place to place by means of round pieces of wood fastened to their sides, yet in Knossos these land-ships were commonplace, some being hauled by teams of oxen as tame as dogs and smaller ones by strange grey long-headed animals with pointed ears and tufted tails. These beasts fascinated Alayne, but at the same time she was wary of them, for they had uncertain tempers and a frightening habit of suddenly giving voice to a noise that sounded like " Ee-aw ! " and when they did this they raised their heads and drew back their lips showing that, unlike oxen, they had teeth on both upper and lower jaws. Even stranger were the small animals that some of the ladies of Knossos kept as pets, leading them about on silver chains. These had bluish fur and long tails, but hands like human hands, and even their faces were human enough to put Alayne in mind of sad old men.

She had been brought to Knossos in a litter borne by four slaves and the journey from the harbour had taken the better part of a morning since ahead walked Leucoperses, the great white aurochs, and progress was impeded by the huge crowds that turned out to see him. The deputy shipmaster walked beside the litter and when they reached the Palace he had given her into the care of a woman so stately and imposing that at the time Alayne had thought she must be the queen of Knossos. Since then she had learned that Raidne — for that was the woman's name — was merely in charge of the girls who lived in the Palace and she was glad that she had not obeyed her first impulse, which was to go down on her knees to this impressive lady who wore flounced, gold-trimmed skirts reaching to the floor, gold ornaments in her hair and a necklace of pearls at her throat.

She took Alayne up to the girls' suite and into a small room which she indicated was to be Alayne's and hers alone, although at first the girl from Dort could hardly believe her good fortune. For the room was a miniature paradise. Its walls were painted with frescoes of dancing youths and maidens, charging bulls, strutting peacocks and swooping eagles, there were goblets made of gold whose only function was to hold great sprays of flowers, and when you opened the shutters of the window you found yourself looking across green meadows to the sea. There were cedar-wood chairs furnished with soft cushions and a curious four-legged article of furniture that Alayne guessed was for sleeping on, but the miracles were only just beginning and before the sun set on that first day so much had happened to her that, when at last she was permitted to slide between the sheets of her strange new bed, she felt she had lived a whole year in the course of a few hours. She had had the first warm-water bath she'd ever had, slave-girls had washed and dressed her hair, her finger-nails and toe-nails had been filed and polished, she had been clothed in a dress almost as fine as that worn by Raidne and finally Raidne had taken her out to a roof-garden where the other girls were eating and drinking . . .

Yet what was the point of it all? That was what she asked herself continually. Why had she been seized and brought to Knossos to be treated partly as a princess and partly as a prisoner? That she was a prisoner was certain, and it was made quite clear to her when she had only been in the Palace two or three weeks. She had been alone in her room, sitting by the window, when the sight of a distant ship putting out to sea had caused her an almost overwhelming spasm of homesickness. For all she knew, the ship might be sailing to Dort, and then it occurred to her that it might prove easier to get home than she had ever supposed. The harbour was not more than an hour's walk from Knossos and, if she visited it, might she not chance upon mariners who had been to Dort and could speak a little of its language? Some might even recognise her for the Pendragon's daughter and believe her when she told them that, in payment for her passage home, her father would reward them with lands and cattle enough to make them rich men for life.

What was to stop her? She gazed down upon the streets of Knossos where women and girls, all dressed much as she was, moved about freely, pausing to chat with their friends or to buy fruit and sweetmeats from the kerbside pedlars. She would have to make her escape during the day, since she knew that the city-gates were closed between sunset and sunrise, and she decided to carry out a preliminary investigation right away.

She left her room, exchanged smiles with two slave-girls who were scrubbing the landing and made for the staircase. No one stopped her. On the floor below she had to slip past a group of grey-bearded courtiers, but they were too intent on their discussion even to notice her, and the second staircase brought her to ground-level. Ahead lay an open doorway leading into a courtyard, and on the far side of the courtyard was one of the Palace gateways.

She never reached it. She never even reached the courtyard

for, as she made to go through the doorway, two slim, smiling young men clad only in gaily-coloured loin-cloths, stepped out from the shadows and barred her way, and in their hands they

carried great bronze double-axes. They smiled at her, shaking their heads and the taller of them pointed firmly towards the staircase, indicating that she was to return to her quarters.

So she was a prisoner, and little by little she had to resign herself to the idea that she might never again see Dort. While she was on the ship she had cherished a belief that presently the warriors of Dort and Sarm would pounce upon her captors and rescue her, but it was a hope that died as soon as she saw Knossos in all its greatness. Why, there must be more people living in just the city alone than in the whole of Sarm and Dort put together, and all about the city lay villages and settlements as far as the eye could see . . .

There was nothing for it but to accept things as they were, and presently she found herself fitting quite easily into the routine laid down for her. She did not understand the purpose of most of it, but none of it was particularly difficult and some of it was quite enjoyable. Each morning she was wakened at dawn by a slave-girl bringing her milk, honey and bread, and after a little while the slave-girl returned to dress her and help her with her toilet. Then, with the other girls, she was given instruction in the language of Knossos and sometimes this lesson was taken by Raidne and sometimes, surprisingly enough, by Daphne, who, it seemed, had come to Knossos already able to speak its language.

Later, they were given other lessons, differing from day to day. Painting and drawing were taught them by a little wizened old man who, apparently, had painted many of the Palace's murals, Raidne instructed them in sewing and embroidery, and another lady, sharper-tempered and more impatient than Raidne, tried to teach them how to play a weird stringed instrument, but the sounds it made were so different from anything Alayne thought of as music that she made no headway and disliked those lessons more than any.

The afternoons were given over to games and athletics. The games, played with balls, hoops and tops, struck Alayne as being childish — there was one especially pointless game that involved tossing wine into a goblet without spilling any — but she enjoyed the athletics. She was the strongest of the girls and could beat all of them at wrestling and all except Daphne at running and jumping.

She was good as well at what their instructor called " bull-leaping ". For this they had a life-sized representation of a bull made of wood and leather and they were taught to vault over it in a variety of complicated ways, one of the most elaborate

of which consisted of grabbing the bull by its horns, then somer-
saulting along its back to be caught by one of the other girls
standing beyond its tail. This manoeuvre seemed to have great
significance, but, while Alayne enjoyed the applause that greeted
a successful somersault, she could not see what was so extraordinary about it nor understand why the people of Knossos
were so obsessed by bulls in every way. You saw paintings of
them everywhere. The chalice from which you drank the sacred
wine at sundown was shaped like a bull and so was the ewer
from which they poured water over your hands before and
after meals ; and, according to Daphne, even the stone prongs
that surmounted many of the Palace walls were supposed to
represent bulls' horns.

She puzzled over the matter constantly and cast her thoughts
back to an entertainment that she and the others had been taken
to during her very first days in Knossos. She had guessed that
it was part of the Summer Festival that Apulu had spoken of,
but now her memory of it was confused and blurred by all the
other new impressions that had been heaped upon her at the
time. She remembered chiefly an open grassy space surrounded
by wooden benches arranged one above the other and packed
with crowds of gaily-dressed people. The stifling afternoon had
given her a headache, made worse by the roar of the crowd and
the noisy music, and she had understood no more of the spectacle
taking place below her than that it consisted of a strange and
exotic form of bull-baiting. There were many bulls, all of them
very young, frisky rather than savage, and amongst them danced,
leapt and vaulted teams of youths and girls, doing more expertly
the very things that she and her companions were now learning
to do with the dummy bull. The performance had been decorative
rather than bloodthirsty. None of the bulls had been injured
and only one of the dancers — a young man who was knocked
over and badly gored, even killed perhaps, but Alayne could
not be sure since he had been at once covered with a sheet and
carried from the field amidst the boos and execrations of the
crowd.

Long before it was time to return to the Palace Alayne had
become bored by watching a sport she did not understand,

but at the very end of the afternoon there were some minutes of solemnity that she remembered clearly. Then, when all the bulls and all the dancers had departed, a fanfare was sounded on a single trumpet and this brought the whole concourse of people to their feet to stand in a silence so heavy that you could almost feel it pressing against you.

There was a second fanfare and the gates at the field's far end opened to admit Leucoperses and his grooms. The great beast was led slowly round and the crowds gazed upon him as awed and silent as if they were watching the passing of a god. Even Alayne was impressed by the sight, yet she could not help wondering what her companions would say if she could tell them that only a few days before she had humbled that great gleaming brute and had rendered him as helpless as a lamb . . .

Many weeks had passed since then, yet Alayne still understood very little more of what her hosts expected of her and presently, in spite of her decision to accept life for what it was, there came a day when she could not prevent herself from rebelling. It happened during a music-lesson. The music-teacher, more than usually irritable that morning, lost her temper with Alayne, mocked her in front of the others and pressed the girl's fingers so fiercely to the strings of the lyre that she almost broke the skin. Alayne did not understand all that the woman screamed at her, but when she cried : " Now try again ! You're not the first ignorant savage I've taught to play the lyre, and if I could succeed with the others, I can succeed with you ! " Alayne at least understood the words " ignorant savage " and her response was to fling the lyre to the ground and walk away.

She heard a shocked gasp from the other girls, but her mind was made up — she had had enough of music, painting, sewing and playing silly games and the sooner her teachers realised it the better. Perhaps if she refused to co-operate at every point, they would give up in despair and send her back to Dort.

She went to her room and threw herself on the bed. Trembling with anger and humiliation, she started to frame some of the things she would say to Raidne when she saw her. At noon she heard the bell that announced the midday meal, but she did not move. She was hungry, but she was also on hunger-strike and she wanted Raidne to know that she was quite serious about her rebellion.

Yet Raidne did not visit her and centuries seemed to creep by before at last she heard the girls come down from the roof-garden, laughing and talking. Then Daphne came in, carrying a bowl of fruit.

" You must be hungry, Alayne," she said, nervously. " Raidne told me to bring you this."

" I'm not hungry," snapped Alayne, " and you can tell Raidne I wouldn't eat that old fruit even if King Minos himself begged me to ! "

Daphne looked shocked and frightened, almost as if she were going to burst into tears. " Well, may I leave it here ? "

" No, you may not ! " said Alayne stoutly, but she was relieved when Daphne put the bowl on the table and sat down on the bed.

" Please, Alayne ! Eat some fruit, and then let's go to the gymnasium."

Alayne ignored the invitation and, propping herself up on an elbow, grinned at the older girl. " Daphne, what happened after I walked out this morning ? "

" We've been forbidden to talk about it," said Daphne, worriedly. " Oh, why did you do it ? Don't you see, you've put us all in peril ! "

" What do you mean ? "

" Can't you understand ? When the Earth-shaker sees that even the King's maidens rebel against their teachers, he will see that the King is without power and so bring Knossos down in ruins ? "

" I don't understand," said Alayne. " You'll have to say it again, slowly."

Daphne did so, and this time Alayne understood the words but was really none the wiser.

" What is the Earth-shaker ? " she asked.

Daphne stared at her wide-eyed. " You really don't know ? " she gasped. " Are there no priests in your land to tell you ? Have you no mother ? "

" I have a mother, but I've never heard of the Earth-shaker."

" You've never heard of the great bull that bears the whole

world on his horns and who can bring cities down in ruins with a single shake of his head ? "

" Not another bull ? " said Alayne, laughing. " Daphne, I'm not a little girl to be frightened by tales of dragons and monsters ! You're talking nonsense. Listen, if there is an Earth-shaker, why doesn't he sometimes shake the earth ? "

" But he does ! "

" Then why don't we feel it ? "

" Alayne ! Have you never known the earth to roar and shake, bringing down walls and houses, and opening chasms in the ground ? "

" Of course not ! "

" But three summers ago where were you ? . . . Alayne, the walls of Tiryns, my native city, are as strong as any in Knossos, but during the terrible heat-wave of three years ago the Earth-shaker, irritated by the heat, gave his head a single shake and made a crack in our North Wall wide enough to drive an ox-cart through ! "

Alayne was beginning to think that everyone in Knossos was mad, and since clearly she couldn't change Daphne's mind about the Earth-shaker, she tried another line of argument.

" Well, even if there is an Earth-shaker," she said, " I can't for the life of me see why he should be interested in my refusal to play the lyre."

" Because he's for ever watching for any sign of disobedience to the King ! Can't you understand ? "

" Not really."

Daphne frowned in her struggle to explain. " Listen — the Earth-shaker is imprisoned beneath the earth, bearing its weight on his horns, and all the cattle in the world are his servants. As long as we keep them in subjection, making sport of them, feeding upon them, drinking their milk, using them to plough our fields, to draw our carts, the Earth-shaker knows that we are more powerful than he is, but any sign of dis-obedience to the King rejoices his heart and invites him to try his strength . . . "

She broke off as a bell rang to summon the girls to the gym-nasium and, getting up, added : " Now come along, Alayne !

Let's go down to the gymnasium together . . . "

Alayne shook her head vigorously. " No, I'm not coming ! Only tell me one thing before you go."

" Quickly, then."

" What will they do if I go on refusing to take lessons ? Will they send me home ? "

" No, by Zeus ! " exclaimed Daphne, then, stooping, she took Alayne's hands in hers and added, very seriously : " Listen, dear — unless you come to table this evening and drink the sacred wine, your bond with King Minos will be broken, you will forfeit his protection and you will be thrust into the Labyrinth to propitiate the Earth-shaker ! "

Labyrinth ? Propitiate ? Before Alayne could ask what the words meant, Daphne was gone, leaving her with a great deal to think about. She helped herself to an apple from the bowl of fruit and carefully rearranged the bowl to look as if it were untouched. Then, eating the apple, she thought over all that Daphne had told her.

She found one thing to cheer her. Daphne had said that sometimes the earth shook and trembled. Alayne knew that that was nonsense, so why shouldn't all the rest of it be nonsense, too ? No, they were simply trying to frighten her into submission, but she was made of sterner stuff than they realised. She would never submit and in the end they would understand that there was nothing to be done except to send her back to Dort. As for the Labyrinth, she couldn't imagine what it was, but she wasn't the girl to let mere words distress her.

She fell asleep during the afternoon and did not wake up until she heard the bell ring for the evening meal.

She was ravenous and she was off the bed and half-way from the room before she remembered what had happened. Then it came back to her and she returned slowly to the bed and sat down on it. She tried to steel herself not to take another apple, but failed, and as soon as she had eaten it, she took a pear, and then another apple.

In fact, she ate all the fruit and, gazing out of the window, gloomily watched the sun sink towards the horizon. It was at sunset that the girls drank the sacred wine and, remembering what Daphne had said, she knew there was still time to retract and give up all idea of rebellion, but she set her jaw more firmly and thrust the temptation from her.

She moved from the bed as darkness slowly filled the little room and paced the floor anxiously as she waited for one of the slave-girls to bring her her night-things and a lamp, but no one came near her and presently she heard the other girls making for their rooms and bidding each other good night.

Later still, she heard Raidne going her rounds, moving from room to room, extinguishing the lamps and wishing each girl happy dreams, but she ignored the rebel altogether. Alayne heard the rustle of her dress as she passed the door, then, as she descended the stairs, the sound grew steadily fainter until nothing broke the silence except the measured tramp of the sentry on the Palace ramparts.

Alayne flung herself on to the bed and buried her face in the pillow, but she had slept too much during the day to sleep now and she had no idea how long she lay there in the dark before a faint sound made her lift her head. Then she turned over on to her back, listening.

Lamplight glimmered under the door and she had the impression that two or three people were coming up the staircase. This was something unheard of and she felt a chill of fear run down her spine. No one except Raidne was allowed to visit the girls' suite by night and she only came if one of the girls was taken ill and rang her bell. Yet there were at least three people on the stairs and they were approaching as steadily as if they moved to the beat of a drum.

Their footsteps crossed the landing and paused outside Alayne's door, and she had to bite her knuckles to keep herself from screaming. The door opened, and too petrified to speak, she found herself gazing at a tall black-clad figure, veiled and holding the lamp high. With the veiled figure were two massive women and Alayne recognised them for the slave-women who did the girls' laundry and all the rough work.

That they were known to her eased her tension a little and she managed to find her voice, although it did not sound like hers. " What do you want ? " she whispered, but no one replied and one of the slave-women came to her and, with a sudden movement, caught hold of her arms and forced them back, while in the same instant she clapped a hand as big as a haddock over the girl's mouth.

The other woman was armed with a club such as they used for pounding the linen and she shook it in Alayne's face. " You struggle, young lady, and I'll have to tap you on the head with this," she said, and Alayne managed to nod to show that she understood. In any case, it would have been useless to struggle. Both women were as strong as oxen and then there was the sinister figure holding the lamp, a figure so heavily veiled that Alayne could not say if it were man or woman.

Never, not even during the actual kidnapping, had she been treated with such indignity, and at every moment she expected either Yele or Dort's Great Warrior to descend from the heavens and strike these people dead, but nothing of the sort happened and she might have been a slave-girl rather than a Pendragon's daughter for all her gods seemed to care. The two women tore her dress from her, pulling her hair in the process, and replaced it with a tunic of coarse linen, then one of them hoisted her on to her shoulder with a further threat of violence if she so much as uttered a squeak. Then the veiled figure opened the door and Alayne was carried from the room.

The Palace slept. The sinister little procession passed no one as it descended the stairs and when the ground floor was reached the black-clad figure led the way across the hall and drew aside a heavy curtain that concealed a door. Bolts were forced back, the door creaked open and Alayne found herself breathing cold air that smelt of dampness and decay.

More stairs, endless narrow flights of them. The walls, criss-crossed with the trails of slugs and snails, glistened with damp, toadstools clustered in the corners and the air grew so musty that Alayne thought that she would choke. Suddenly her nerve gave way, all her resolution vanished and she beseeched the slave-woman to set her down. Shadows wheeled through the darkness as the figure bearing the lamp turned and muttered something, and the slave-woman lifted Alayne from her shoulder.

" Let me go back ! " panted Alayne. " I promise I'll — "

The veiled figure silenced her with a raised hand, and said : " The bond is broken — "

" Raidne ! " gasped Alayne. " Oh, Raidne, is it really you ? "

" In this place I am nameless," said Raidne, " as are we all, and your name can never be reclaimed. You, dedicated to the King, have disobeyed those who serve him, you have refused the wine, you have broken the bond . . . "

" I didn't understand ! "

Raidne ignored her, saying : " This is something that hasn't happened in more than twenty generations of men, you have most likely brought disaster upon Knossos, so now go to the Earth-shaker and see if he will save you ! "

Near-panic seized Alayne as she realised the hopelessness of her position, but she managed to control it and Raidne permitted her to walk the rest of the way down the stairs, sparing her the indignity of being carried.

The stairway grew narrower and the stairs themselves degenerated into mere ledges of rough-hewn rock, wet and slippery from the water that streamed down the walls. Then Raidne stopped, raising the lamp, and Alayne saw that they had come to a door in the rock, a door that was encrusted with verdigris and held shut by three great bronze bolts, each as thick as a man's arm.

Years must have passed since the door was last opened. The verdigris had jammed its bolts and corrupted its hinges, and the slave-women needed every ounce of their strength to get it open.

Alayne kept her eyes on Raidne in the hope that she would relent at the last moment, but the older woman, inscrutable behind the black veil, seemed to be without pity, then the heavy door groaned open and Alayne was thrust into the darkness beyond with such force that she stumbled and nearly fell.

By the time she recovered the door was shut, and she could hear its bolts being knocked back into place. The only other sound was that of dripping water, and the darkness was so all-enveloping that she could not say whether she was in a tiny cell or a vast underground hall.

The only object of whose existence she was certain was the door, and she settled herself against it, squatting on her haunches. Strangely enough, now that she knew the worst she was not as terrified as she had been earlier, and she told herself that her one hope of survival was not to allow her courage to fail her. She remembered how her father, wounded, had crawled the whole way from Dort to Sarm, and she was determined not to sell her life more cheaply than he. He had survived with all the odds against him and so, by the grace of Yele and the Great Warrior, would she.

Naturally she was hungry and she knew that the pangs would get worse before long, but she also knew that after two or three days you reached a state in which you were no longer aware of your hunger, and then you could go for at least another week without food. Water, however, was a necessity, and she held her breath as she tried to locate the sound of water dripping more exactly, and eventually decided it was somewhere to one side of her and at some distance.

The next thing was to learn something about her prison. Small stones and fragments of rock lay at her feet and, taking up a handful of these, she threw them from her one at a time in an attempt to locate the walls. Some of the stones seemed to strike rock almost at once, while others travelled for as long as a second before the sound of their impact came echoing back to her, and little by little she drew a mental picture of a small ante-chamber with three, perhaps four wide tunnels leading from it, and she also noticed some slight movement in the air suggesting that somewhere there were other entrances to what she now knew was the Labyrinth.

Guided by the sound of dripping water, she crawled cautiously forward on a journey of exploration, and she marked her course with little piles of stones so that she would be able to find her way back to the door.

# Chapter Nine

IT was very much as Orontes said it would be — for several days the four ships followed the course of the great river eastward and then swung with it towards the south. The river was in flood, the current was strong and progress was slow, but it was not until they were many miles inland that the tribesmen inhabiting the river-banks gave any trouble and then it was only to shoot warning arrows across the ships' bows. The warriors were all for giving battle, but Artor, on Orontes's advice, brought them to heel by threatening loss of rank for any who disobeyed him. He promised them they would see plenty of fighting before ever they returned home and told them to keep their ferocity for their real enemies, Alayne's captors.

He and Orontes had themselves rowed ashore in one of the boats and with them they took a quantity of trade goods, mainly bronze daggers and trinkets, to present to the tribesmen's chieftains and their wives. Orontes explained that these people knew little of bronze since, being fishermen, they had nothing to trade and no traders visited them. On the other hand, they were far from being savages. As boat-builders they were as good as the Rhosmenans, their tribal system was advanced enough to enable one chieftain to rule numerous settlements and they had a system of law. Even so, Artor, remembering the arrows that had been shot towards the ships, felt far from comfortable as the boat neared the shore, and wondered if perhaps the warriors' way would not have been more sensible.

The tribesmen stood silent on the river-bank grouped in a semicircle about a tall old man who was evidently their chieftain, and Artor saw that there were archers amongst them with arrows on their bow-strings. Mostly the men were armed with flint battle-axes and spears, few had swords, but their clothes were of tanned leather and good linen, and the Chieftain wore a fine head-dress made of eagles' feathers.

When the boat was still some way from the bank, Orontes went to its bow and, standing up, held up his hands in a gesture of peace and to show that he carried no weapon. He could speak several languages and in one after another he greeted the Chieftain and assured him that they came in peace. The tribesmen watched him impassively, but when he recited his message in the language of Sarm Artor thought they relaxed a little and certainly some of the archers lowered their bows.

Artor had always been told that, many generations before, the people of Sarm and Dort had come from a land beyond the sea and now it occurred to him that these tribesmen could well be his distant cousins. So he made his way to the bow of the boat and asked Orontes if he might address the Chieftain, for indeed the shipmaster spoke Sarm's language with such a strong accent that sometimes even Artor had difficulty in understanding him.

" Speak by all means, my lord," said Orontes. " Though I doubt he'll understand."

He moved back a little and Artor took his place, while the rowers used their oars only to keep the boat bow-on to the bank.

" Greetings, great Chieftain ! " he shouted, speaking slowly. " I am Artor, only son of the Pendragon of Sarm, a great land lying to the north beyond the sea, and my father sends you presents and greetings . . . "

The tribesmen were listening as if they understood and, with growing confidence, Artor went on : " Great Chieftain, I believe that your people and my fathers are of the same blood, related not more than five or six generations back. My father is also Artor by name . . . Artor, son of Tola, son of Utta, son of Pahto, son of Lanzo, son of Fenyor, son of Ostal — "

He broke off as the Chieftain suddenly raised his arm in a gesture of greeting, and shouted : " Welcome to the land of Liga, Artor, son of Artor ! " . . . and, although he pronounced the words in a strange way, Artor found he could understand him easily.

The Chieftain went on : " We are indeed of one blood, for I am Ostal, Paramount Chieftain of the River People, and I am the great-great-great-great-grandson of the Ostal you speak of, just as your father is. And our bards still sing of that Ostal's son, Fenyor, who went adventuring across the sea with a host of followers to find new lands, and now they may add a new verse to their songs ! . . . *Greetings* ! "

He roared the last word with the full power of his lungs and it was taken up by the tribesmen until the air seemed to tremble with the thunder of their welcome. Spears and axes were flung to the ground as a token of goodwill and Orontes ordered the rowers to row for the bank . . .

No sooner had Ostal taken Artor's hands in his than he commanded a great banquet to be prepared and to it he invited all the warriors from the ships, and Artor's heart sank a little as he saw celebrations being organised on such a scale that they might last days. The warriors were almost as keen about feasting as they were about fighting, and they were also extraordinarily interested in their family-trees. So, with a lavish supply of food and drink, and an absorbing topic of conversation, there was no telling how much time they might not idle away.

Meanwhile, Ostal spared no pains to make his remote cousin feel at home, and in no time Artor found himself installed in the Chieftain's house being entertained by his numerous kin. The house, although shaped like a bee-hive and built of clay and wattles, was as large as any in Sarm, and presently it became clear to Artor that the Chieftain was at least as powerful a ruler as Sarm's Pendragon.

He learned this in conversation with Ostal's eldest son, a young man of some twenty summers. His name was Lanzo, and he and Artor took to each other from the start. Lanzo told Artor that there were many settlements along the river, each with its own chieftain, but all were subjects of the Paramount Chieftain and paid him tribute. " So now that we know your mission is a peaceful one," said Lanzo, " and in no way aimed against our interests, you will have a peaceful journey with all possible assistance from our people."

Artor was a little puzzled by this and wondered if he'd been misled by Lanzo's strange way of talking. " But my shipmaster tells me that the river continues towards the south for many hundreds of miles," he said. " Surely your father's power does not reach to such distances ? "

Lanzo laughed and assured him that it did. " One might almost say, from the mouth of the river to its source," he said. " That is an exaggeration, I know, but the fact is that this stretch of the river, where it runs between low hills, is ideally placed for the imposing of our will — if the up-stream settlements became troublesome we could dam the river and flood their lands, or if those down-stream from us gave trouble we could span the river with nets and starve them of fish. Of course, these things never happen, but the knowledge that they could is enough to uphold the ruler's authority."

That explained a lot about the land of Liga. It explained the source of Liga's wealth — a wealth that became more and more apparent as the preparations for the banquet went ahead — and how it was that Liga was so civilised, although lacking bronze and never visited by the traders. By means of the river the various settlements were kept in constant touch with each other, and no hills or forests could separate them ; and Artor reflected that if only there was a great river linking Sarm with Rhosmena the famous stones could have been moved in half the time.

He told Lanzo of the plan to move the ships overland from one river to the other and smiled when the young man shook his head doubtfully.

" You think it can't be done, my Lord Lanzo ? " said Artor, then went on to explain how the great stones had been moved many hundreds of miles across all sorts of terrain.

Lanzo was interested and impressed, but he still had doubts about Artor's plans, and, when he had heard all about the great stones, he said : " My lord, I have no misgivings over the skill of your artisans, nor should the distance between the rivers prove an obstacle — it is little more than a good day's march — but your route will take you over hills infested by the wildest, most bloodthirsty savages you've ever set eyes on. And you have only a handful of warriors with you. These savages, men and women alike, fight like wild cats · They are constantly raiding the settlements on the upper reaches of the river, but when one marches against them they vanish as if the ground had swallowed them up."

" Have they swords, and other weapons of bronze ? " asked Artor.

" They have not, my lord, but they are expert archers and very skilled in the use of the throwing-spear."

" But surely no match for trained warriors bearing swords ? No, my Lord Lanzo, these savages may harry us, but I doubt if they can stop us moving the ships. Now what can you tell me about the peoples dwelling on the banks of the farther river ? "

" Very little," said Lanzo. " We have no dealings with them, but two men who crossed the mountains some years ago came back with tales of great wealth and luxury, saying that the lords of that river lived in houses built of stone, wore nothing but the finest linen and used bronze even for articles as common as cooking pots."

" Are they a warrior people ? " asked Artor.

" Not in the sense that they live by fighting, my lord," said Lanzo, " but no doubt they would be capable of repelling any foe that tried to take their river from them. Yet we really know nothing about them, for our world ends at the mountains and I am sorry for it. Why, my Lord Artor, I would give my right arm to have a part in your adventure, that I might learn more of other men and lands."

" You would ? " cried Artor. " Then why not come with us ? "

" I ? " asked Lanzo, in surprise. " But what use could I be ? I am no warrior, I know little of ships and I should be nothing to you except an extra mouth to feed."

Artor denied this, thinking how much easier the journey up-river would be if he had the son of the Paramount Chieftain with him.

Before he could say any more about it, Orontes came to him accompanied by two soldiers who bore a heavy wooden chest between them. " Trade goods," murmured Orontes, with a glance at the chest. " I sent to the ships for a few of the best pieces, and perhaps, my lord, you would present them to the Chieftain at the end of the banquet ? "

" I should be most pleased to," said Artor, " but, Orontes, I must admit that I'm rather worried about these festivities. They could go on for days."

" No doubt, my lord, but as to that, I think we shall gain more from the goodwill of these people than we lose . . . and we certainly mustn't give any cause for offence ! "

" No," agreed Artor, and he was about to tell Orontes of a plan he had, when he was interrupted by a herald summoning everyone to the banquet, and one of Ostal's daughters came to him to ask if she might show him to his place.

There were no tables and no benches such as graced the great houses of Sarm, and perhaps this was due to the shape of the Chieftain's house, for all the guests sat on the floor in concentric circles with those of the highest rank nearest the centre, and they were served by kitchen slaves moving between their ranks. As principal guest, Artor found himself on the Chieftain's right, and, with a heavy heart, he knew that he would be expected to make a long speech after the banquet in reply to the Chieftain's official speech of welcome. He tried to compose his speech during the meal, but it was not easy for Ostal was a talkative man, and plied him with questions concerning Sarm and its ruler. As for the food, it was mostly fish for which Artor had no liking, but the wine, served in well-made earthenware cups, was the most delectable he had ever tasted, and Ostal promised to have several skins of it put on board his ship.

The warriors and the tribesmen got along quite as well as Artor had expected they would, and long before the banquet was over the noise was so tremendous that he could hardly hear a word the Chieftain said, and he was decidedly relieved when at last, at a nod from Ostal, the herald leapt into the centre and called for silence.

Familiar with the ways of rulers, Artor was not surprised that the Chieftain's speech took up almost as much time as the banquet itself, and he won the goodwill of the entire company by keeping his own speech very short. He thanked the Chieftain profusely for his hospitality, then hurried on to the business that everyone was waiting for — the opening of the gift chest.

Orontes had selected the presents generously, and gasps of astonishment greeted the objects as they were lifted from the chest — necklaces of gold and silver, jewelled brooches, golden rings and bracelets, bronze swords, bowls and bells. Never had these people seen so much metal in one place, and many of them were gazing at Artor as if he were a god.

More speeches followed, and more toasts, and then the bards took over, singing songs in Artor's honour, so that, with one thing and another, it was well past midnight before he had a chance to resume his talk with Orontes. By then the Chieftain's house was in an uproar, with all the revellers singing at the tops of their voices, and Artor and the shipmaster were able to slip out into the night unobserved.

The moon was at the full, and they strolled down to the river and sat on the bank, while Artor spoke of his conversation with Lanzo.

" He wants to join us," he told Orontes, " and I'm inclined to think that he could be extremely useful. The warriors won't agree to leave here for at least five or six days, so why shouldn't I take the ships' boats and press on up-river with Lanzo as my guide ? I would take the artisans with me, select the best place for beaching the ships, and start making preparations. Then, by the time you arrived with the fleet there would be nothing to do except haul the ships from the water."

" When would you plan to leave, my lord ? " asked Orontes, doubtfully.

" As soon after sunrise as I can."

" But, my lord, you're very young for such an undertaking," objected Orontes, " and you are inexperienced in the ways of ships. Much time would be lost if the place you chose for the beaching wasn't suitable."

" How do you mean ? "

" Well — insufficient draught, or too steep a bank . . . "

Artor protested that he wasn't a fool. " I shall have old Kalsedo with me," he said, " and I'll be guided by him."

The man Artor spoke of, a Rhosmenan, was the chief of the artisans. Sailor turned shipbuilder, he had devised the great rafts and sledges that had been used for moving the blue stones, and Merwun the Sage was among those who thought that the stones would never have reached Sarm had not Kalsedo been in charge of the operation. " The idea originated with your father," Merwun had once told Artor, " and I was able to give a great deal of advice, but when, ten thousand summers hence, men still gaze at these stones, Kalsedo is the name they should honour " And here was Orontes suggesting that Kalsedo didn't know enough to beach a few ships !

Artor drew a deep breath, conscious that they were trying an issue which had so far never been put to the test — which of them, when it came to a difference of opinion, was really in charge ?

He said : " Do you really think that Kalsedo doesn't know enough to take the ships' draught into consideration ? "

" Of course not, my lord, but — "

" Go on," said Artor.

" I'm thinking of the warriors, my lord. What power have I to make them obey me once you have gone ? '

" None," agreed Artor, " but I shall make every one of them swear on the ring of Sarm to embark five days after I leave. Once they have sworn, they will give you no trouble."

Orontes was still not entirely convinced, but he had the habit of obedience, and when he said : " Very well, my lord, if that's what you've decided," Artor knew that his authority would never again be questioned, and he felt as if he'd suddenly become a man.

He didn't go to bed at all that night, but had a talk first with Lanzo and then with Kalsedo, and told them of his plans, and by the time dawn broke the four ships' boats had all been provisioned and prepared for the journey. Each of the boats had places for four oars, and so that the journey could continue day and night, Artor decided to take thirty-two rowers with him. They were hand-picked men, chosen for their strength and endurance, and each was promised his freedom if he acquitted himself well. The artisans would also be expected to help with the rowing from time to time, and a sailor was allocated to each boat to act as helmsman.

The day dawned with a light mist hanging over the river,

and it promised to become a scorcher. Artor assembled the yawning warriors on the river-bank and had every one of them kiss the ring of Sarm and promise not to prolong his stay beyond the fifth day.

Then, amidst the cheers of tribesmen and warriors, the little flotilla set off, moving slowly against the current.

By the time the mist cleared, the boats were out of sight of the settlement, and it was then that Artor, surveying the wide, silent river, began to doubt the wisdom of his venture. Every minute carried him deeper into a foreign land, and so eager had he been to assure his hosts of his peaceful intentions, that he had not brought a single archer or warrior with him. The artisans were unarmed except for the tools of their trade and the flint knives they wore at their belts, and in any case they were a mixed bunch, owing no allegiance to Sarm, and working for anyone who would provide them with food and clothing.

In his anxiety to lose no time, Artor had put himself entirely in the hands of the river people which would be all right provided they were as friendly as Lanzo said they were, but which would be disastrous if they proved hostile.

Then, glancing at Lanzo out of the corner of his eye, he decided that his suspicions were misplaced. No one could have a more honest or cheerful face than Lanzo, and Artor was relieved to notice that he did not carry even so much as a dagger.

The sun rose, and soon the sweat was running down the rowers' shoulders in torrents, but they were in high spirits, happy in the knowledge that they were working for their freedom, and Artor noticed that they rowed even better than when they had the overseer's lash at their backs. It seemed presumptuous to question the ways of the traders, yet he found himself wondering if they were right to depend so much on slaves, and soon he was dreaming of an ideal world in which no man could own another as if he were an ox or a sheep. He saw himself as the ruler of such a world, and there was no telling where his thoughts might not have taken him had not Lanzo broken the silence by laughing and asking him what he was dreaming about.

" Nothing much," said Artor, " but I wish a wind would rise, that we might hoist the sails and make faster progress."

" I think we're better off without a wind," said Lanzo. " At this time of the year it would probably come from the south or south-west, and make things even harder for the rowers. But don't worry, my lord. We shall reach our destination within six days, as I promised."

It was not just a matter of rowing steadily against the stream for hour after hour. At some points the river flowed through deep gorges, hemmed in by towering cliffs, and at those places the current was so strong and the rocks so dangerous that it was impossible to use the oars as anything except punting-poles, and on the second day one of the boats overturned with the loss of most of its provisions. Fortunately the boat itself was saved, together with its crew, but once again Artor found himself awed by the magnitude of the task he'd undertaken.

Farther south conditions improved. The river broadened, the current grew almost negligible, and one whole day was spent with the rowers and artisans wading in the river close by the bank and towing the boats through water not more than an arrow's length deep. Sometimes tribesmen lined the banks to watch the little flotilla pass, but Lanzo's presence was a guarantee against trouble, and at every settlement he was greeted by oak branches held aloft in acknowledgement of his authority. In fact, the natives were just as friendly and peaceable as he had said they would be, and long before the boats reached their destination Artor had forgotten his qualms.

Towards noon on the fifth day of the journey, mountains began to be discernible at some distance from the eastern bank of the river, and Lanzo told Artor that it was hereabouts that they should disembark.

Artor consulted with Kalsedo, who was in charge of the leading boat, but the old man was gloomy and told him that he could hardly have chosen a worse place.

" Cliffs," he said, pointing to the shore, " and for some miles now the river-bottom has been strewn with boulders and jagged rocks. Also, my lord, there are few trees in these parts, and we shall want great quantities of timber for our purposes."

" But there are some trees," said Artor. " Surely enough to make a few rollers."

" We shall need much more than just rollers," said Kalsedo, " and, my lord, unless we go about our task in the right way, we shall most certainly fail."

The old man was adamant. There was nothing for it but to accept his advice, and for the rest of that day the four boats continued to struggle up-stream without him finding a suitable landing-place.

Towards evening, Artor ordered the boats to be beached and a camp to be made. This was the first time he had done so, but there could be no point in continuing the journey by night and perhaps missing the ideal place for hauling the ships ashore. At any rate the rowers were glad of the rest, and the chieftain of the nearest settlement presented the expedition with some cold venison and wild pork and several skins of wine, which made that evening's meal almost a feast.

Before Artor turned in that night he had a long talk with Kalsedo, since he wanted to make sure that the old man was not just being pig-headed and, in particular, he couldn't see why so much timber would be needed. He said : " Kalsedo, you moved the great stones over vast stretches of country using nothing but rollers, so why can't you do the same with the ships ? It isn't as if you'll be short of labour. If the rowers and the artisans aren't enough, the Lord Lanzo says that we can enrol peasants and fishermen from the neighbouring settlements."

" It's not a question of labour, my lord," said Kalsedo, " and I must respectfully point out that stones are one thing and ships are another. Ships have to be kept upright, and if we hauled them over rollers without protection we should do so much damage to their keels and garboards as would take half a year to put right."

" Then what do we do ? " asked Artor.

" Why, my lord, we make great cradles by lashing spars together, and it is within these cradles that the ships will travel. I have all the necessary measurements here in my head, and we can start work just as soon as we come upon a sizeable spinney of pine trees."

" Then the cradles will move over rollers ? "

" Just so, my lord. In all we have a labour force of some three hundred men, and with half of them moving the ships by haulage and leverage, and the other half shifting the rollers from the rear of the procession to the front, we should be able to make very fair progress. If these two rivers are not separated by more than a day's march for an unburdened man, we should not take more than half a month to make the same journey. I am told that the main pass through the mountains is quite easy to negotiate, and that there are no really steep places either coming or going."

" Where did you get this information ? " asked Artor.

" Why, my lord, from one of the rowers, who lived as a boy in those very mountains. He was captured while taking part in a raid upon one of the settlements on the farther river and sold into slavery. He is a rough and savage man, my lord, but I have no doubt that he knows those mountains like the palm of his hand."

" Have him brought to me," said Artor.

Night had closed in by the time the rower was located and brought to Artor, but the moon was rising and there was just enough light for Artor to realise that the man was as big as any he had ever seen. He had black ringlets down to his shoulders and a great black beard that almost concealed his features leaving no more than an impression of flashing eyes and powerful white teeth. His name was Polda, and he spoke a dialect that bore enough relation to the language of Sarm for Artor to be able to understand him with Lanzo's help. He was a man of over forty, and Artor gathered that for twenty-five years he had been a slave, lashed to a ship's oar.

" I'm told you come from these near-by mountains ? " said Artor. " And I'm told that your kinsmen are famous for their cunning and ferocity."

" As ferocious as wolves and as cunning as snakes," agreed Polda, grinning amiably, " and when we get to the mountains they'll set me free. Then, you'll be the slave, and I'll be the lord."

" You're asking for a flogging," said Artor, taken aback by the man's boldness. " Men have been lashed to death for less than you've just said."

" Lashings are meat and drink to me, my lord," laughed Polda. " How else do you think I came by my health and strength ? Not by ships' food, I can promise you."

Artor responded to the man's good humour, and decided to overlook his bluntness.

" These kinsmen of yours," he said, " are there many of them ? "

" Thousands, my lord," said Polda. " They're as numerous as the waves of the sea."

" Thousands ? " echoed Artor. " Are you trying to tell me that those bare mountains can support people in their thousands ? "

" No less, my lord. Why, in my tribe alone there are five times more people than I have fingers and thumbs, and my tribe is only one of six, equally large."

" Say, about three hundred souls in all, including women and children," laughed Artor. " Why, Polda, what became of your thousands ? "

" I have no head for these things, my lord," said Polda, " but everyone of my kinsmen can take on ten ordinary men and defeat them, be they armed with swords, spears, battle-axes or even thunder and lightning."

" My lord, he always talks in that vein," put in Kalsedo. " But when you question him closely you find that his kinsmen are half-starved, and the mountains only large hills. I don't think that either the men or the mountains will give us much trouble."

" No ? " asked Polda. " Then, old man, your surprise will be that much the greater."

" Tell me, Polda, about the people of the farther river," said Artor. " How do they compare to your kinsmen ? "

" They're like gods," said Polda. " Otherwise, how do you think I came to be captured ? They live in stone houses, dress only in linen, and wear as much gold and silver about their persons as King Minos himself. You see, my lord, for many many years they traded with the men of Knossos, but now all that is passed."

" How so ? "

" Why, some twenty summers ago the traders of Knossos carried off one of their high-born maidens, and the offence has never been forgiven. Now booms span the river-mouth, and the very name of Knossos is a curse and an insult."

This was interesting news, and questioning Polda closely, Artor learned that the men of Knossos were hated in almost every land that bordered the inland sea.

Said Polda : " My lord, I can hardly name a land that hasn't lost at least one prince or princess to the bulls, and many times I have helped row ships carrying the victims to Knossos."

" Lost to the bulls ? " queried Artor. " What does that mean ? "

" I cannot tell you, my lord. Such mysteries are beyond the understanding of a mere slave of the oar who has never been nearer Knossos than the harbour."

It seemed certain that Artor would not lack for allies, but it was the question of time that troubled him mostly. There was so much to do, and so little time to do it in, and his relief was enormous when, only an hour after embarking next morning, they came upon a perfect landing-place. There the river-bottom was of gravel, it sloped gently up towards the river-bank, and between the river and the foothills there lay a stretch of grass-land as lush as any in Sarm ; and to the south, less than half a mile from the landing-place, there was a small forest of pine trees, so exactly suited to Kalsedo's purposes that it was as if Yele himself had put them there.

# Chapter Ten

IT was strange how quickly Alayne became used to the total darkness, and before she had been in her prison an estimated two days she was counting the darkness as the least of her discomforts.

Almost unbearable were her hunger-pangs, but thirst was no problem for she soon located an underground stream filled with cold, fresh, fast-running water. At first she had hoped to find a way out of the Labyrinth by following the stream but in this she was disappointed. The stream had its source in an underground spring, and after running for some way through the Labyrinth, disappeared eventually beneath a flat rock poised hardly a hand's breadth above the floor of the cave.

Alayne explored the Labyrinth tirelessly, keeping track of her movements by means of little heaps of stones and always returning to the great door which she knew led into the cellars of the Palace. Her bed was a heap of small stones, and she measured the passing of time by thinking of her spells of sleep as night, and her periods of activity as day.

Four tunnels led downwards from the area of the door, and one of these Alayne found particularly interesting since, from its depths, she sometimes heard faint sounds such as the lowing of cattle and men shouting. It seemed to act as a whispering gallery to a quite different part of the Labyrinth, but although Alayne explored the tunnel for a distance of five thousand paces, the sounds never seemed to grow any louder nor the darkness any lighter. Still, she persevered, and presently started a systematic exploration of all the smaller tunnels that branched from the main one.

It was on the fourth or fifth day that the miracle happened, and it came just when her spirits had reached their lowest ebb.

For hour after hour she had been crawling through the Labyrinth's tunnels, getting nowhere, and feeling so faint that the slightest movement seemed to call upon every ounce of her strength, and when at last she got back to the area of the door, she was closer to despair than at any time since leaving Sarm. Then, as she flung herself on to her bed of stones, her foot brushed against something that she could not immediately recognise. She put out a hand, and for a moment thought she was suffering from hallucinations as her fingers touched first a coarse blanket, and then, wrapped in the blanket, a large chip-basket in which were three or four jars, a loaf of bread and several small packages wrapped in vine-leaves. Alayne's head swam with excitement, and she would have fainted had she not broken off a piece of the loaf and crammed it into her mouth. Never had any food tasted more delicious and, gloating a little, she carefully opened each of the jars and the packages.

Her unknown benefactor had been generous. One of the jars contained wine, and the others were filled with honey and olives, and wrapped in the vine-leaves were pressed figs, cheese, some almond-and-honey sweetmeats and a large lump of raisin cake, while at the bottom of the chip-basket were several handfuls of walnuts.

It was necessary for her to taste all the food to find out what had been sent, and she noticed that none of it was particularly perishable, which suggested that some time might pass before her friend in need could bring any more. She realised she would have to ration herself very strictly, and then fell to wondering who her benefactor could be. She wondered if Raidne had been suddenly moved by pity, but decided it was unlikely. Daphne was a possibility, but there were several things against it. Neither the bread nor the cheese was of the sort served to the girls, while the blanket was as coarse as if it were woven from goat's hair, and she had never seen one like it in the girls' suite. It put her in mind of the blanket that the men of Knossos wore over their shoulders in wet weather and on cold evenings, but the only man the girls ever met was the old drawing master and Alayne could not think that he would interest himself in bringing her provisions.

There seemed to be no answer to the riddle and presently she gave it up, wrapped herself in the blanket and fell into a deep sleep, hugging the chip-basket against her to keep it away from any rats that might be scampering about the Labyrinth.

Even more important than the food itself was the knowledge that not everyone had abandoned her, and now she slept more soundly than at any time since the great door had closed upon her.

On waking, she found herself reluctant to leave the area of the door in case her well-wisher returned, intending to help her escape, and for the next few days she hardly moved except to pay the briefest of visits to the underground stream for the purpose of obtaining fresh water and washing herself. She filled the long empty hours by telling herself stories, and kept herself in good spirits by reflecting upon the deeds of the ancient heroes of Dort and Sarm, reminding herself that they had endured and survived far greater ordeals than any that had so far fallen to her lot — so far she had at least had no trouble with dragons and neither had any magician appeared to turn her into a toad or weasel.

She was a strong-willed girl and kept very strictly to her rationing system which was to eat a little bread, cheese and honey upon waking, and a few walnuts and olives before going to sleep. Half-way between these two meals, as nearly as she could judge it, she allowed herself two or three mouthfuls of cake or sweetmeat, and she still had nearly half her original provisions left when she heard a sound that brought her to her feet in an instant.

One of the bolts on the great door was being stealthily drawn back !

She tiptoed to the door and waited, hardly breathing, with her heart thumping like a trip-hammer, until the second bolt was withdrawn.

The door groaned open and a ray of pale, flickering light, the first she had seen in she knew not how long, cut the darkness. Her eager whisper : " Who is it ? " produced no reply except a muffled exclamation of surprise, and in the same instant a basket was thrust roughly into her hands and the door closed with a thud so uncompromising that Alayne had to struggle to keep back the tears.

The basket contained an even greater quantity of food than the first one, but Alayne was more upset than grateful. For a fleeting moment she had glimpsed the world beyond the darkness, a flickering rush-light, a young man's frightened face, and then the vision had vanished as abruptly as if it had never been. She could not even put a romantic interpretation upon the incident. It would be pleasant to think that the young man was secretly in love with her, but she had to admit that his behaviour was hardly that of a lover. Even the most timid suitor would have exchanged a few words with her, and this young man had simply behaved as if he wanted nothing to do with her at all. But if so, why had he come ? And who was he ? Almost certainly he was one of the guards of the lower courtyard — no one else would have access to the cellars — but why should he risk his life to bring her food, and then behave so strangely ?

In any case, it seemed quite certain that the young man did not intend to help her to escape, so there was nothing for it but for her to resume her explorations in the hope of finding a way out of the Labyrinth.

She decided to penetrate farther into the most promising of the tunnels than ever before, spending, if necessary, two or three days about it and, with that in view, she packed all the food into the larger of the baskets, put the blanket round her shoulders and set off.

The first part of the journey was easy. She was beginning to know all the twists and turns of the tunnel quite well and the route was well-marked with stones. As she made her way forward she counted her paces, and in her heart she thanked old Merwun the Sage for all the trouble he had taken to teach her her numbers. At the time it had seemed quite pointless, and she had had to put up with a great deal of teasing from her friends. Who, they asked, had ever heard of a girl learning to count beyond twenty — or needing to? — and she had felt much the same about it herself. It was her mother, the Lady Morva, who had insisted upon her acquiring an education, and she had told Merwun to give Alayne no peace until she could count to ten thousand as easily as most people counted to ten.

Perhaps it was her imagination, but the noises echoing along the tunnel sounded louder and more insistent than usual. Most of the noise was made by cattle, and they sounded as if they were expecting a thunderstorm. They lowed continuously and there were even moments when she could hear the rustle of straw and a faint rasping as the animals rubbed themselves against rubbing-posts. It was difficult to believe that they weren't sharing the darkness with her, but she knew that sound behaved strangely in caves and as a little girl she had been taken to Kedda to see and hear its famous whispering gallery. She remembered putting her ear against the cave's rough wall and hearing Artor speak softly to her although he was more than half a mile away . . .

At last, almost exactly on her five-thousandth pace, she came to the large heap of stones that marked the limit of her explorations so far. She was tired and hungry, and she decided to have a meal and a sleep before going farther. Actually she was too weary to eat much and, after a few mouthfuls of bread and a little wine she wrapped herself in the blanket and fell into a deep sleep, with her head pillowed on the heap of stones. Dreams plagued her, and some of them had such an element of terror that they were almost nightmares. All the events of the past few weeks became jumbled in her sleeping mind, and over and over again she dreamt that she was running away from unknown pursuers through forests, caves, mazes and similar places, and each time she outdistanced those who sought to capture her, she found her way barred by Leucoperses, the great aurochs bull.

At first, whenever that happened, she managed to escape him by half-waking up and shifting her position, but later on, as her sleep became heavier, the hold exercised by the dreams over her mind became harder to break, and then there was no easy escape from her nameless pursuers, nor from the great bull that stood awaiting her, bellowing and stamping his feet at the end of a tunnel.

In her dream she stumbled and fell then caught one horrifying glimpse of Leucoperses as he lowered his head and came charging along the tunnel with such force that she could actually feel the ground tremble beneath her . . .

She awoke, bathed in sweat and with a scream on her lips, and the relief she felt upon finding that it was only a dream was at once swamped by an appalling discovery — the ground she lay on actually was trembling !

She freed herself from the blanket's enveloping folds and was struggling to sit up when a noise far louder than the loudest clap of thunder she'd ever heard, burst upon the darkness, and the ground started to rock and shake so crazily that she could not have got to her feet even had she wanted to.

All about her she could hear the crash and thud of falling rock, and every sound echoed and re-echoed through the tunnel as if the whole world had dissolved into noise, and Alayne, in spite of her terror, remembered what Daphne had told her and found one explanation for the disturbance — the Earth-shaker ! The monstrous bull, who, dwelling in the bowels of the earth, had only to shake his head to bring whole cities down in ruins. Perhaps already Knossos was no more !

The cattle were stampeding. Mingled with the other sounds, Alayne could hear the thunder of their hooves as they plunged this way and that, bellowing in terror, and she could hear men shouting at them and sounding almost as terrified as the bulls.

Her terror affected her sense of time, and she could not have said whether the upheaval lasted minutes or hours. She only knew that it stopped almost as suddenly as it had started, and it was followed by a silence so profound that she could well have believed herself to be the only living creature on earth.

Even the cattle were silent, perhaps had all been crushed to death by falling rock, and for a long time Alayne was aware of no sound at all except the thumping of her heart.

Fear of the repetition of the earthquake rendered her almost helpless and for a long time, unnerved and trembling, she stayed where she was, sitting with her arms clasped about her knees and gazing into the darkness.

Later, she realised that she was very hungry and, as she made a meal of bread and olives, some sense of her identity returned to her and, reminding herself that she was Alayne, daughter of the Pendragon of Dort, she reproved herself for her abject behaviour and pulled herself together. Then her impulse was to return to the area of the door and she could guess that it would not be easy. She could be sure that in some places the roof of the tunnel had collapsed, and she was prepared to find that many of her heaps of stones had been disturbed and scattered.

With the food-basket on her arm and the blanket about her shoulders she started out and progress was exasperatingly slow, since common sense told her that she should test the ground at every step in case a chasm had opened up in her path. The condition of the tunnel was even worse than she had imagined it would be. In many places the walls had caved in and the fragments of jagged rock that covered the floor cut and bruised her feet. Dust hung in the air and made its way into her eyes and nostrils and throat, and she dared not drink more than an occasional sip of wine since she could not tell how long it would take her to reach the stream, or if, indeed, the stream would still be there. Mice and rats scurried through the darkness, squeaking in dismay at the damage that had been done to their familiar haunts, and several times the Labyrinth was shaken by faint, echoing tremors. Whenever this happened Alayne flung herself to the floor of the tunnel in case that monstrous, subterranean bull took it into his head to shake the earth again.

Another part of the tunnel hardly seemed to have been disturbed at all, and for a little while she made good progress, moving rapidly from one of her little heaps of stones to the next, but just when she was beginning to think that she would get back to the area of the door without much trouble, she found herself faced by the worst obstacle so far. A great section of the roof had crashed down into the tunnel, blocking it almost completely.

In falling, the great mass of stone had crushed part of the tunnel's wall, reducing it to powdery rubble and Alayne set to work shifting enough of this rubble to enable her to by-pass the obstacle. The one thing that kept hope alive was a draught of air whistling among the broken stones, since it at least suggested that the tunnel was not blocked for an interminable distance.

Little by little, working until her fingers were sore and bleeding, she cleared a space wide enough for her to squeeze into, and she found the next stage of her task nerve-racking in the extreme since, as she dislodged the loose stones, she continually risked bringing down a cascade of fragments that would knock her over and bury her. As she worked she used the blanket as a sack, filling it with rubble and then dragging it back into the clear part of the tunnel, and this took up even more time than the actual digging.

She couldn't have said how many hours she spent trying to scrape a passage-way round the rock, but she worked without pause, not even stopping for food or drink, working mechanically and reaching such a point of exhaustion that she began to hear imaginary voices and in particular someone calling her name. When that happened she decided it was time to stop, and she crawled wearily back through the passage-way and threw herself on to a heap of rubble. She was almost too weary to eat, but she drank a little wine, and was in the act of dipping a piece of raisin cake in honey when, quite unmistakably, she heard her name called again. " Alayne ! . . . Alayne ! "

The cry was very faint, as if it came from a great distance, but it was no hallucination ! She was sure of it, and scrambling to her feet, she cupped her hands round her mouth and answered the shout with a single word : " Here ! " She hurriedly swallowed some more wine, made her way along the excavated passage-way to its end, shouted two or three times more, then set to work again in a frenzy, pausing only to answer to her name each time it was called.

The draught of air was stronger now. She could feel it on her sweat-damp face and arms, and the next time her name was called it sounded a great deal nearer.

" I'm here ! " she shouted in reply. " You're coming in the right direction ! "

She was sure now that the voice was that of a woman, and a few minutes later, she glimpsed something that made her laugh for joy — a faint glimmer of light shining through the crevices of broken rock.

" You're so near I can see your lamp ! " she shouted. " Where are you ? "

" Alayne ! The tunnel's blocked . . . "

Incredibly, the voice was that of Raidne, but before Alayne had time to consider what this might mean, the last of the rubble collapsed, and tumbling forward with it, she realised that she had skirted the obstacle.

Faint, dancing light filled the tunnel and, as she picked herself up, she discovered that Raidne was about a hundred paces away, painfully scrambling over fallen debris.

Alayne hurried towards her, and the older woman, holding the little lamp high, gazed at her almost as though she was seeing a ghost. Her expression was a mixture of relief and shock. Then she threw a cloak round Alayne's shoulders and gave her a hug.

" I've some little cakes here — " she began, but Alayne shook her head, and explained that she was too excited to eat.

" Too excited ? " gasped Raidne. " But you've had nothing to eat for ten days ! "

Alayne decided that it would be better to say nothing about the baskets of food, and simply mumbled something about her hunger-pangs having passed off.

" Shall I be allowed to leave the Labyrinth now ? " she asked.

" But, of course ! Why do you think I came ? "

Alayne shrugged, and shook her head dumbly. Too much had happened to her in too short a time, and although there were a score of questions running through her tired brain, for the moment she wanted no more than to be allowed to bath and go to bed . . .

# Chapter Eleven

THAT summer there was a total eclipse of the sun, and it was visible in most of the lands that bordered the inland sea. Soothsayers almost everywhere saw this as a bad omen for Knossos, and when presently they heard that a great earthquake had destroyed more than a third of the city they felt that their predictions had been fulfilled.

Here and there, however, there were kings and petty rulers who were not entirely happy with their soothsayers' interpretation of the eclipse — who thought that perhaps their own authority was about to be endangered — and amongst them was the ruler of the upper reaches of that river towards which Artor and his host were struggling so slowly and painfully. His name was Marso, and he had cause to be anxious, for almost daily reports reached him suggesting that the mountain savages were on the warpath.

He was a young and vigorous ruler, and during the five years of his reign he had done a great deal to keep the savages at bay. He had built strong stockades around all the principal settlements, he had established a system of outposts to give warning of imminent raids, and he had trained a body of scouts to penetrate into the mountains and find out what they could of the savages' movements. Now they were sending him reports of continuous warlike activity. The savages were dancing their war-dances day and night, and the tribes were gathering together on an unheard-of scale.

Marso's territory was not rich enough to support a class of trained warriors. Most of his subjects were peasants and fishermen, and they were scattered over too wide an area to be able to beat off a really determined attack on the part of the savages. Marso remembered the eclipse of the sun, read into it the collapse of his rule, and came very close to despair.

"I am paying the price of my youth and inexperience," he told his chief adviser, who was a Greek from Mycene. "In my father's time, hardly a full moon went by but what the savages raided one settlement or another, but we survived. I put an end to the raids by taking strong measures — and with what result? Why, the savages, starving and desperate, make peace among themselves and combine to attack us on a greater scale than ever before . . . Well, Tisander, you are probably wiser and certainly older than me, so what is to be done?"

Old Tisander, with more experience of life than his master, did not take quite so gloomy a view of the situation. He said: "My lord, these savages, though they be as numerous as the hairs of my beard, can never be more than a rabble. Five hundred trained warriors could put them to flight in an hour."

"I dare say," agreed Marso, "but we haven't got five hundred warriors. We haven't got five."

"I'm thinking of your kinsman, the Lord Kancho. He has warriors, and to spare . . ."

"Him!" exclaimed Marso, scornfully. "Come, old Tisander — is your brain softening? Why should Uncle Kancho lend me any warriors? And even if he did, how should we ever get rid of them again?"

King Kancho ruled the lands lying at the river's mouth, and he was known to be extremely rich and powerful. His wealth he had inherited from his forebears who, in turn, had obtained it by trading with Knossos, Mycene and Egypt, and his power derived from an army of several thousand warriors and a fleet of nearly a hundred ships, although they were mostly small. His warriors were said to be little better than brigands, and his sailors little better than pirates, but there was no doubt that Kancho could command their loyalty.

"As a citizen of Mycene," said Tisander, "I have even more reason than most to distrust allies, but, my lord, I don't think you would have anything to fear from your uncle. He would have seized this stretch of the river before now had it been in his interests to do so — "

" Hear, hear ! " interrupted Marso. " At least you don't mis-judge the old villain ! "

Tisander smiled, and went on : " On the other hand, my lord, he would be loath to have this territory in the hands of a rabble of mountain savages. They would be a constant threat to his rear, hindering him in the prosecution of these grandiose adventures he's always planning."

" Yes, that makes sense. Then what do you advise ? "

" Why, my lord, that you send a messenger to him on the very next tide, telling him that the savages are on the warpath. Request that he sends a force of about five hundred warriors and pay him the compliment of asking him to command them himself."

" Will you act as messenger ? " asked Marso, and, when the old man agreed, gave his consent to the plan . . .

The next few days were anxious ones for Marso, and when the wind was in the west the settlements could hear the throbbing of the savages' war-drums.

The only encouraging scrap of news brought in by the scouts was that the savages had not yet started to paint themselves, and since they never carried out even the smallest raid except in full war-paint it seemed unlikely that they would attack just yet.

Meanwhile a message arrived from King Kancho, to say that he was marching north with five hundred warriors for whose services Marso would be expected to pay in corn and salmon.

Marso had hardly received that message when the most experienced of his scouts reported to him with an extraordinary piece of news. This man, whose name was Flonda, could speak the savages' dialect with some fluency and, according to him, the warlike preparations were not aimed at the river settlements at all. By pretending to belong to a distant tribe, Flonda had managed to attend one of the war-dances as a spectator and there he had found all the tribesmen talking of a mysterious people who had sailed up the great river on the far side of the mountains and were now about to invade the mountains them-selves.

" From all accounts," said Flonda, " they came up the river

in ships as large and fine as those of Knossos itself. Yet their warriors wear neither shoes nor caps and have the look of northerners."

" Have they swords of bronze ? " put in Marso.

" Yes, my lord, and other weapons of bronze as well. Spears, battle-axes and daggers."

" Flonda, I think you must have misunderstood your informants. Why should such men trouble to come great distances merely to war with a few half-naked savages ? "

" My lord, I have more to tell you," said Flonda, patiently. " It seems that these warriors brought a number of craftsmen with them as well as sailors and rowing-slaves, and when the ships reached a certain point of the river they were hauled ashore one by one. And now, my lord, those four ships are being slowly dragged on rollers towards the mountains."

This Marso could not believe, and laughing, he clapped his scout on the shoulder. " Flonda, you're a fraud," he laughed. " For years you have been telling me that you could understand the savages' language, and now I find that you only think you can. Why, man, your common sense alone should tell you that ships and mountains simply don't go together ! "

Flonda looked hurt, and stubbornly insisted that he had understood the tribesmen correctly. He said : " My lord, to my way of thinking, those people whoever they may be, are not merely taking the ships to the mountains, but intend to bring them to this river — "

" But why ? " asked Marso. " Why, why, why ? Tell me that, old fraud ! "

" My lord, I can do no more than guess," said Flonda, " but sailors have told me that the only way into the inland sea from the west is by way of Herakles's Pillars, and those straits are guarded by the ships of Knossos. Therefore, my lord, might not certain enemies of Knossos, seeking to enter the inland sea, sail up one river, cross the mountains and sail down another ? "

" Enemies of Knossos ? " murmured Marso, his interest caught at last. " Then they must be very determined and bitter enemies indeed if they think they can defeat King Minos with four ships and a few dozen warriors. Well, Flonda, we shall see what we shall see, and if in the near future I notice four ships sailing over yonder mountains you shall be suitably rewarded. Otherwise I must arrange to have you held under water for an hour or two to cool that feverish imagination."

" My lord, I haven't added to what I heard by so much as a breath."

" I believe you," said Marso, looking anything but convinced. " And you say that the savages have no intention of attacking us whatsoever ? "

" I'm sure of it, my lord. They have set their hearts upon capturing those ships, which they believe to be laden with treasure of all kinds. Their plan, as I understand it, is to delay the attack for as long as possible, in the hope that their enemy will weaken himself by his exertions."

If Marso had his doubts about Flonda's story, they were nothing to those expressed by King Kancho when he arrived a few days later. He came by boat, accompanied by Tisander and a handful of retainers, and the five hundred warriors, travelling overland on foot, were not expected for another three or four days.

Kancho was a noisy, corpulent man, renowned for his huge nose, and when Marso told him about the four ships crossing the mountains he nearly burst his body-armour with laughing.

" Ships as large as those of Knossos ! " he gasped, wiping tears of laughter from his eyes. " Why, ships of that size can't be moved over rollers for any distance. Even if they didn't break their backs they'd start to shake to pieces before they'd travelled a hundred paces. Well, well, well ! What will you think of to tell me next ! You know, you and your man Flonda must be a couple of ignorant bumpkins to have believed that tale even for a moment ! "

" That's all very well, Uncle," said Marso, struggling to hold his anger in check, " but Flonda's no fool. He's a reliable man and an honest one. He doesn't talk for the sake of hearing the sound of his own voice."

" Oh, I know all about that, my boy," said Kancho, " but

don't you see ? For once, the savages outsmarted him. His disguise didn't fool them for a moment, but instead of using him for archery practice they decided to stuff him full of nonsense and let him come back to you. You know, to lull you into a false sense of security ! "

Marso knew that it was useless to argue with his uncle, so he tactfully changed the subject and asked him how he proposed to deal with the savages.

" We'll attack ! " roared Kancho. " I've no use for defensive tactics, and we'll attack just as soon as we can deploy our forces. I want you to round me up about a hundred peasants and set them to work making a forward camp in the lee of the foothills. Nothing elaborate, you know — just a stockade behind which we can keep our supplies of food, water and arrows."

King Kancho might be overbearing and conceited, but he was not a man to let the grass grow under his feet, and by the time the warriors arrived he had made extensive preparations for the campaign. The stockade had been built, tents had been pitched and the settlements had been coerced into supplying great quantities of meat, fish and grain.

The forward camp faced the main pass through the mountains, and Kancho planned to send a body of about two hundred warriors into the pass, while the remainder, divided into two groups, infiltrated into the mountains to the north and south. These men would be guided by Marso's scouts and they would take up their positions before the other warriors set out, with the intention of attacking the savages in the rear once the battle in the pass was joined.

" It will be all over in a matter of hours," the old man assured his nephew. " A few untamed savages, armed with flint hatchets, are no match for trained warriors bearing swords."

Marso did not feel quite as confident as his uncle, but when the warriors arrived he had to admit that he had never seen a finer-looking body of men. Every one of them was more than six feet tall, and with the sun shining on their helmets and breastplates, they looked more like the gods and heroes Tisander had told him about than mortal men, and when their king explained what was required of them they seemed almost amused by the easiness of the task.

" Why, my lord," said their senior officer, " any fifty of us could have done the job, but we're all grateful to you for the chance of a morning's sport."

Marso was not himself a warrior and the presence of these arrogant, blustering fellows made him uneasy. They were polite enough to his face, but round the camp-fire that evening he noticed certain of them sniggering amongst themselves and glancing at him askance, as if they were telling each other that there sat a man who believed that ships could sail over mountains, and a little later he managed to have a brief talk with Tisander about it.

" These braggarts have only been here half a day," he remarked, " and already they behave as if they owned the territory. Do you still feel certain that we can get rid of them at the end of the campaign ? "

" I'm sure of it, my lord," said Tisander. " During the journey up-river, the king took me a great way into his confidence, and if only half of his fine plans come to pass he will need every one of his warriors to help him."

Marso laughed. " He still sees himself as a rival to King Minos, does he ? "

" Not quite that, my lord," said Tisander, also smiling. " But I gather he's joined the secret alliance that seeks to bring the men of Knossos to their knees. He tells me — "

The old councillor broke off abruptly as the royal herald approached them to invite them to take wine with the king in his tent . . .

Marso, unused to tents, slept badly that night, and he was up and about well before dawn, still wrestling with the problem that he'd spent most of the night considering. Tisander was probably right when he said that these five hundred warriors would withdraw as soon as the campaign was over — but might they not one day return and seize his lands ? His uncle was powerful and he was weak, and he had not the means to raise an army. On the other hand, with King Kancho straddling the river-mouth like a colossus, Marso's land could not grow rich by foreign trade. It was quite a dilemma, and little by little his thoughts drifted in the direction of the peoples dwelling on the other side of the mountains. He knew little of them, but, if King Koncho's warriors gained a decisive victory over the savages, might not the pass be opened up to trade? And might not an alliance be formed?

Thinking these thoughts, he sat himself upon a rock and gazed down into the pass just as the day's first light reached it. There was no mist that morning. The air was as clear as crystal, and presently, as the light grew stronger, Marso became aware of something moving in the pass's far distance. At first it was little more than a low-lying dust cloud, but Marso had the eyes of a hawk, and by staring fixedly in that direction he was gradually able to resolve the movement into its details.

At the head of it marched a dozen or so tall men — warriors, certainly, for he could see the rising sun's red light glinting on their swords — and then came two parallel groups of men who all leaned forward as though they were hauling on ropes. It was these who were disturbing the dust, and between the two groups other men scurried to and fro as if they were placing objects on the ground, one in front of another.

Suddenly Marso understood and then, in the depths of the dust cloud, he could discern a tangle of lashed spars enclosing what was undoubtedly the hull of a great ship . . .

# Chapter Twelve

ARTOR and Lanzo, as befitted their rank, travelled as passengers in the leading ship, and if they lived to be a hundred they didn't suppose they'd ever experience a stranger journey.

As the vessel, lashed firmly upright in its pinewood cradle, trundled over the series of rollers, it plunged and rocked as if it were sailing over a choppy sea, and from the towering poop-deck the young men could get a fascinating bird's-eye view of the whole operation.

When matters went well, the four ships moved forward in an unbroken line, with hardly an arrow's-length separating the stern of one from the bow of the next, and the whole procession was not much more than three hundred paces long — that's to say from nose of the foremost haulage-slave to the back of the last man in the rearguard of warriors.

To keep the progress continuous the tracks of rollers had to be twice as long as the length of the four ships together, and the slaves, whose task it was to shift the rollers, had to work at it harder than Artor had ever seen men work. From dawn to dusk they had to move at the double, plucking up each roller as soon as the ships had passed over it, racing up one side of the procession for some distance beyond the leading ship in order to lay the roller again, and then running back empty-handed along the other side to the rear once more.

Naturally, matters did not always go well, and the early stages of the extraordinary journey had been marred by a whole series of accidents — ropes had broken, men had fallen beneath the cradles, and one of the ships had rolled on to its side by breaking loose from its lashings. Then, four days had been lost while the slaves filled in a dry gully to enable the procession to pass over it, and even more days had been lost in clearing rocks from the path of the ships, but since crossing the watershed progress had

been remarkably steady and at least the calamity that Artor
dreaded most of all had not come to pass — the mountain savages
had not launched an attack. By now it seemed unlikely that they
would do so, for the day that was just dawning would take the
ships beyond the mountain area, and then there would be
nothing except open country separating them from the second
river.

Artor and Lanzo were in high spirits as they sat on the poop-
deck and breakfasted off bread and dried fish, and Artor remarked
that they'd certainly come by one good story to recount to their
sons and grandsons.

" Probably no one else in the world will be able to say that
he once crossed a range of mountains on board ship," he pointed
out.

" No one except you and I and the poor wretch with the broken
legs in the hindmost ship," agreed Lanzo. " Still, we must
congratulate ourselves upon casualties being so light. One man
killed, one injured, is not a bad showing."

" Far better than I'd dared hope for," said Artor. " Had the
savages attacked, how much blood might we not have shed ? "

Suddenly shouts rent the dust-laden air and the cradled ship
lurched to an abrupt stop.

" Look out ! We're off the rollers ! " cried Artor, and grabbed
hold of the nearest rope to steady himself. It was rare for a day
to pass without one or another of the ships running off the
rollers, and when that happened it was usual for the ship immediately behind to ram it. Artor and Lanzo had taken some
nasty falls before they became familiar with the signs, but by
now the clutching of the nearest rope or rail had become almost
automatic.

" The whole procession's stopping ! " said Lanzo, and then
the two of them made their way cautiously to the rail and peered
down through the spars and lashings.

Everyone seemed to be shouting, and there was too much
dust in the air for Artor to be able to see anything clearly, but he
had the impression that the haulage-slaves were falling back
while most of the warriors were making their way forward. He

caught sight of old Kalsedo and shouted to him asking him what was wrong.

" The warriors of the vanguard have called a halt, my lord," replied Kalsedo. " They say we're threatened."

" Savages ? " asked Artor.

" I think not, my lord. The warriors speak of men wearing helmets and breastplates."

Artor had heard enough, and he hurried towards the ladder and started to clamber down it, closely followed by Lanzo. He jumped from the ladder's bottom rung into a struggling mass of slaves, sailors and warriors, but two or three of the warriors recognised him and quickly cleared a space with the flats of their swords.

" An army faces us, my lord," said one of the warriors. " The vanguard has called us all forward."

" Have the slaves fall back and let us through," commanded Artor. " And somebody find Orontes."

Precious minutes slipped by while they fought their way to the front of the procession, and as it was Artor reached the vanguard only just in time to prevent some of the more hot-headed warriors charging up the path with drawn swords and yelling war-cries. He ordered them to put up their swords, then turned to the vanguard's captain, who was a staid, sensible warrior of the second degree.

" Well, Gervor ? " he asked. " Whence comes this report of a hostile army ? "

Gervor pointed to a couple of archers and explained that he had been using them as scouts.

" They say that there's a force of some two or three hundred well-armed warriors spanning the mouth of the pass some eight thousand paces from here. They're supported by peasants with bows, and to the rear of them is a stockaded encampment."

Artor felt himself go cold. " Two or three hundred warriors ! " he muttered.

" Yes, my lord. With more in reserve, most probably."

" Then we'd be very foolish to try conclusions with them. We must parley."

The fiercer of the warriors groaned at this and muttered amongst themselves, but Artor ignored them and turned to Lanzo.

" Do the men on this side of the mountain speak a language similar to ours ? " he asked.

" They do not, my Lord Artor. In fact, travellers have told me that their language is more like the barking of dogs than human speech."

This was discouraging, but Artor squared his shoulders and remarked that he would have to do his best with signs and gestures. Then he ordered the two archers to find him some evergreen boughs such as he could carry as an emblem of peace and, unbuckling his dagger, handed it to Gervor, who looked startled and incredulous.

" My lord, do you intend to go amongst them unarmed and unescorted ? " he asked.

" Why, yes. How else can I convince them of my good faith ? "

" My lord, I implore you to take a handful of us warriors to serve as a bodyguard. The enemy facing will count as nothing a leader who comes towards them unarmed and without a retinue."

" These men aren't our enemies as yet," said Artor, " nor need they be if we act circumspectly. After all, we want no more of them than safe passage to their river, and for that indulgence we can reward them with presents of bronze, silver and gold."

However, he was far more nervous than he sounded. The grumbling of the warriors undermined his confidence and when a few moments later the throng parted to make way for Orontes, Artor could hardly have felt more relieved had the shipmaster been his own father.

" Come, Orontes, and talk some sense into the heads of these fire-eaters," he said by way of greeting, then went on to outline the position in as few words as he could, only to be disconcerted at the end by Orontes shaking his head.

" My Lord Artor, the warriors are right," said the old ship-master. " You would be ill-advised to approach these foreigners entirely alone, yet I think it would be equally wrong for you to take warriors with you bearing swords."

"Then who?" shouted one of the warriors. "You, I suppose?"

"I was about to suggest it," said Orontes blandly, "if only for the reason that I may be able to speak these men's language, or one akin to it."

Several of the warriors muttered doubtfully, and the one who had spoken before shouted: "Oh, and no doubt as a ship-master of Knossos you'll wear your blue cloak. That should invite a hail of arrows for a start."

"I think not," said Orontes. "The cloak will catch their interest, certainly, but they'll hesitate to pick a quarrel with the might of Knossos until they know our intents and purposes."

There was a moment or two of silence, then Lanzo turned to Artor.

"I, too, would come with you, my Lord Artor," he said. "It is likely that the ruler of these men knows my father's name, and at least the two peoples have one bond between them — a common enemy in the treacherous savages that infest these mountains."

"A fine idea!" shouted the noisy warrior, sarcastically. "Who better to represent us than a foreign sailor and two boys!"

"And a dog!" put in another warrior, pointing to Polyxo who lay crouched at Orontes's feet, and the laughter that greeted this sally made Artor flush with anger.

"My lords, hold your peace!" he shouted. "My mind is made up and you have but two courses open to you — one is to accede to my orders as you once swore to do on the ring of Sarm, and the other is to strike my head off. Well?"

The silence his words produced was deeper than before, and no one looked up as the two archers returned bearing some parched-looking pine branches. Then Gervor gave an embarrassed cough and said, shuffling his feet: "My lord, our obedience is assured, even though you command every man of us to fall upon his sword. We honour your courage in approaching these strangers unarmed, and we only questioned your decision out of our regard for your safety."

That ended the incident, and Artor would have been happier in its conclusion had he been perfectly sure that he was right and the warriors wrong, which he wasn't. Still, it was too late to draw back now, so taking one of the evergreen branches he set out along the pass, with Orontes on one side of him and Lanzo on the other.

" Is Polyxo to come with us ? " asked Orontes, with a glance at the white dog.

" Why not ? " said Artor. " There's something about a dog that disarms enmity — even as ferocious a one as Polyxo."

By now the sun was well above the horizon and, dazzled by its glare, Artor could see very little of what lay ahead. The heat oppressed him, and as he trudged over the rough rock-strewn ground his self-confidence seemed to diminish with every step.

No one spoke much, but presently Polyxo began to growl and whimper as if he were scenting something hidden from the humans. His attention seemed to be drawn towards the summits of the low, jagged cliffs that flanked the pass, and when Artor looked towards the cliff-top he fancied he saw a slight movement as of a man hurriedly withdrawing from sight. A few paces later he caught sight of a man's head and part of a bow silhouetted against the sky, then knew that they were advancing under the scrutiny of an unknown number of archers.

His palms sweated coldly, but there was nothing to be done except march steadily on and hope that none of the archers succumbed to a sudden urge to test his marksmanship.

Orontes suddenly came to a standstill, shading his eyes.

" There they are, my lord," he said. " A host of warriors, as well accoutred as any I've seen in Knossos."

Artor and Lanzo also pulled up and gazed towards the mouth of the pass. They could see them as tall, motionless figures, dark against the green of the plain beyond, and Artor was amazed by the amount of metal they carried, for not only did they wear helmets and breastplates, but had armour on their thighs and legs, and each had a round bronze shield strapped to his left forearm.

" They are giants," he muttered. " Every one of them is taller than the tallest man in Sarm."

Orontes laughed a little uncomfortably. " They are big men, certainly," he said, " but at least some of their height they owe to those great plumed helmets."

" Perhaps," said Artor, " but if these are the warriors of an outlying land, what can the warriors of Knossos itself be like ? "

" By no means so formidible," Orontes told him. " The men of Knossos are a seafaring people and rely upon ships to defend them rather than warriors."

When less than fifty paces separated Artor and his companions from the warriors, a trumpet suddenly blared, a word of command was shouted, and Artor felt himself flinch as an arrow whistled through the air and half-buried itself in the dust fewer than ten paces ahead of them.

" So they want us to stop," murmured Artor. " Now what happens ? "

The three of them stood there, holding their pine branches aloft and squinting into the sunlight.

From the ranks of the warriors came another trio of whom only one wore armour, and he looked as if he could take on whole armies single-handed. He had the chest of a bull, his arms were thicker than most men's thighs, and his huge nose might have been intended for the prow of a ship — he looked the sort of man who could march through stone walls without ever noticing them.

At his side there walked a much younger man clad in green and white robes, and although he was built on a slighter scale, he bore about as much resemblance to the warrior as a son might bear to his father.

The third member of the party was a gentle-looking greybeard clad in white robes and he walked two or three paces behind the others as if he were of inferior rank.

When the three men came to the half-buried arrow they

halted. The bulky warrior drew his sword with a flourish and gave tongue to a string of words that sounded sufficiently like the barking of dogs to make Polyxo prick up his ears and growl, and when the warrior broke off as if waiting for an answer, Artor glanced at Orontes.

" Do you understand him ? "

" Not a word, my lord," said Orontes, and addressed the warrior in his own tongue, that of Mycene and Knossos.

If the warrior didn't understand him it was clear that the greybeard did, and he addressed his companions, presumably asking for permission to speak. This was granted and then there followed such an animated exchange between Orontes and the greybeard that they might have been lifelong friends.

Orontes turned to Artor. " My lord, good fortune smiles on us," he said. " This old gentleman and I are both from Mycene, and we have acquaintances in common. His name is Tisander, and he is chief adviser to the ruler of this land — "

" The fat warrior ? " put in Artor.

" One might suppose so," said Orontes, " but, in fact, it's the other gentleman, and his name is Marso. The warrior, who is called Kancho and styles himself King, is his uncle, and the ruler of extensive lands to the south. Also, these warriors are his liegemen and are under his command."

" I see," said Artor. " Then convey my greetings to both the rulers, and tell them I ask no more of them than permission to haul the ships to the great river and thus gain access to the inland sea."

Both uncle and nephew seemed somewhat suspicious of the request when it was translated to them, and Orontes said : " King Kancho wants to know your purpose in going to the inland sea."

Artor hesitated. " What think you, Orontes ? " he asked. " Shall we tell them that we seek to right a wrong committed by the men of Knossos ? "

" I think so, my lord. The slave Polda has told us that these people have no love for Knossos."

" Go ahead, then."

This time the reaction of the two rulers was very different, and King Kancho gave a great shout of understanding. Then he sheathed his sword and came towards Artor with outstretched hands, talking so much and so loudly that Orontes and Tisander had great difficulty in keeping up with him.

" In brief," said Orontes, " the King is saying that any enemy of Knossos is a friend of his, and he invites the three of us to take wine with him in his tent."

King Kancho was not an easy man to impress, but during the course of that morning it became clear that he was full of admiration for a people who could move great ships across mountains, and he admitted that in the whole of his fleet he had no ships whose size could compare with those of Knossos.

He talked too much and too volubly for the interpreters to be able to convey more than the gist of what he said, but Artor was not slow to see that the four ships were his greatest asset, and he instructed Orontes to make the most of them.

" I'm doing so, my lord," said Orontes, " and now I learn something of great interest. You know that all along I have been expecting to find allies in the inland sea in the form of certain refugee noblemen of Mycene ? "

" Yes, of course."

" Well, it seems that under the leadership of a man who calls himself Zagreus, matters have prospered greatly with them, and now their headquarters are on a great island some four or five days' journey by ship from King Kancho's dominions. Apparently, this Zagreus, although physically tiny, is a man of enormous energy and brain-power, and he has succeeded in welding all those rulers who have suffered at the hands of Knossos into an alliance intent on revenge. His plans are well advanced, and King Kancho is ready to wager that the power of Knossos will not survive another year."

" A year ! " exclaimed Artor. " But you yourself said that we must rescue Alayne before the Winter Festival ! "

" And I hold to that, my lord," said Orontes. " For that reason we must get to this Zagreus with all possible speed. You see, we can present him with an argument that can make a huge difference to his timing. This summer we have an advantage such as will never come our way again."

" What do you mean ? "

" Simply this. The four ships we have in our hands will be expected by the men of Knossos to return at the end of summer. We shall be able to sail straight into the harbour without question, and with a company of warriors hidden aboard each we could, as it were, unlock the door for the rest of Zagreus's forces."

Artor could see that it would constitute a powerful argument, but he had to leave it for the moment to raise his chalice to King Kancho, who, flushed and boisterous, was toasting him for the fifth or sixth time. In fact, the conference was growing quite convivial, and Lanzo and Marso, with the help of Tisander, were having a great time comparing conditions on their respective sides of the mountain range.

Naturally, conversation in almost any direction was difficult, and King Kancho was in the act of offering to sing a war-song when from outside the tent a trumpet suddenly blared and produced an immediate change in the royal mood. His smile became a scowl, and in the same moment his personal guard entered the tent and addressed him rapidly.

The King's reaction was to seize his sword, shield and helmet, shout a few words to Tisander and dive from the tent.

" The savages, my lord ! " exclaimed Orontes, when Tisander had interpreted. " They're attacking the ships in force ! "

Outside the tent all was uproar as the warriors hurried to re-form their ranks, and Artor, through the two interpreters, asked Marso if weapons could be found for him and his companions. Marso nodded and left them, and then there was a nerve-racking delay during which Artor could do nothing except wait by the tent and watch the warriors as they charged from the encampment in the direction of the pass.

A page came to them bearing battle-axes. Artor took the first that came to hand, then set off with Orontes and Lanzo pounding along at his side.

Dust-clouds as thick as fog hung in the air, and the sound of battle reached them long before they could see anything of it. Mainly they heard the shrieking war-cries of the savages, and Artor had a mental picture of the wild men pouring down the cliffs in their thousands.

As Artor and his friends entered the pass, the whistle of arrows greeted them and Artor, glancing up, had a dim impression of hand-to-hand fighting going on along the cliff-tops as the savages sought to oust Marso's peasant archers.

An arrow tore skin from the back of Artor's neck, and not many seconds later the dog, Polyxo, suddenly described a ghastly somersault with an arrow through his breast. Orontes went on his knees beside the animal and was about to lift him, then realised it was hopeless.

" Dead, my lord ! " he panted. " Right through the heart ! "

Great boulders came hurtling down from the cliff-tops. One struck a warrior just ahead of them and brought him down so precipitately that Lanzo tripped over him and fell headlong. Artor and Orontes helped him up, then turned to raise the warrior, but he had broken his neck and was dead.

Lanzo, knowing little of swords and their significance, would have taken that of the fallen warrior, but Artor, shocked, forbade it, and, as they pounded onward along the pass, explained that no man other than a warrior might use a sword, and that even he, although a Pendragon's son, might not bear one until he became a warrior.

" Even in battle," panted Lanzo, " may not a man pick up a dead warrior's sword ? "

" No, Lanzo, not even to save his life."

" It's a . . . bit silly, isn't it ? "

" Absurd, but there it is. The warriors are a jealous and touchy lot, and would lop off a man's head rather than see him infringe their rights."

An ear-splitting war-cry thundered along the pass, and Artor guessed that the front ranks of Kancho's warriors had joined the battle. The tremendous noise they made raised his spirits and stirred his blood, and now he could just discern the hull of the foremost ships looming through the clouds of dust. It was growing hot and he was bathed in sweat, but he was in good condition and in spite of the great distance he had run he was breathing almost as easily as when he left the camp.

Ahead, the pass was choked with a mass of struggling men, and now Artor could make out the forms of naked savages as they swarmed up the networks of spars enclosing the ships. No doubt they were trying to get at the trade goods that lay in the ships' holds, but someone had had the sense to order certain slaves aboard the ships and they were using the great sweeps to knock the savages from the spars.

This was Artor's first experience of battle and he was disconcerted to find everything so muddled and confused. For a long time he could not get anywhere near the heart of the battle. There were too many of Kancho's warriors ahead of him, and as more still came he soon found himself caught, surging back and forth, in a press of frustrated men, each of them eager to get at the enemy and prove his mettle.

However, those minutes he spent locked among the warriors gave him some chance to form a picture of the battle as a whole. The savages — and there were some hundreds of them certainly, if not the thousands he had visualised — had broken the ranks of Sarm's warriors and were now massing fairly solidly around the ships, fighting off counter-attacks launched by the warriors they had displaced.

On the fringes of the battle sailors, artisans and slaves were harassing the savages with whatever weapons came to hand — boulders, rollers, working tools and flint axes captured from the enemy.

The savages' women lined the cliff-tops hailing stones and rocks into the mêlée, and every now and then a huge boulder came thundering down, crushing whomever lay in its path, be he attacker or defender.

Then, as the savages were forced back from the leading ship, the battle opened up so abruptly that Artor, taken by surprise, lost his balance and would have fallen had not Orontes, appearing from nowhere, caught him by the arm and steadied him. In the next instant they were separated again by the eddy and swirl of the battle, and now that the resistance of the savages was cracking, a frenzied wildness seized the warriors. Artor found himself carried forward as by a wave, until another group of warriors, surging in at right-angles, forced him back against the spars of the second ship.

Then he was amongst savages, and fighting desperately, swinging the battle-axe to and fro as he strove to keep a zone of safety between himself and the blood-crazed tribesmen. He caught one of them a blow on the jaw that would have killed most men, and indeed these creatures, fearsomely painted, hardly seemed like men, and it was easier to think of them as beings from another world. To make themselves the more repulsive they had daubed their bodies with the flesh of fungi — stinkhorn and the like — and in the heat of the morning the reek was so offensive that several times Artor thought he was about to faint from nausea.

His enemies were armed with sharpened deer's antlers and short-handled flint axes, so that in the matter of reach he had the advantage of them, but sooner or later they must have pierced his defences had not four or five warriors pounced on them from the rear, scattering them and then pursuing them.

The centre of the battle had moved on down the pass and Artor was glad of the respite. He wiped the sweat off his face with his forearm and took stock of the position.

Now the fighting was around the third and fourth ships, and there seemed little doubt that the warriors were getting the better of it.

The women had deserted the cliff-tops as if they knew that the battle was lost, and all around were the wounded and dying. Slaves moved amongst them, succouring the friend and finishing off the foe, and Artor caught sight of the giant Polda and wondered how it was that he hadn't deserted to his kinsmen. He was about to go to him when a dark shape sprang upon him from amongst the spars and bore him to the ground. In his astonishment he dropped the battle-axe, then felt the hand of his attacker close upon his throat. In the savage's other hand was a flint hatchet, and he was in the act of bringing it down when

Artor caught his wrist and gave himself a few moments' longer lease of life. More than that he could hardly hope for, and already waves of darkness were surging through his head as the savage's fingers bit deeper and deeper into his throat.

Gathering all his remaining strength he made a supreme effort to throw the man from him, but it was hopeless, and as the savage jerked his wrist free, Artor, gasping and retching, screwed up his eyes in anticipation of the final blow.

But it never came. Instead, Artor heard a crunching thud. The pressure on his throat relaxed, and he opened his eyes to see the savage topple over sideways with blood cascading from his head.

Artor heaved himself away from the dying man, and looking up, saw his deliverer silhouetted against the sky, roaring with laughter and still wielding the great roller with which he had killed the savage.

It was Polda ! Polda, the truculent slave who had said that when they reached the mountains he would be the lord and Artor would serve him. And now the huge fellow put out a hand and helped the boy to his feet.

" How are you, lord ? " he bellowed. " That was a narrow escape you had, and by the look of it that throat of yours will be black and blue for a month ! "

Artor could hardly speak. He was rubbing his throat and struggling to express his thanks when Orontes came running up.

" Thank heavens you're safe, my lord ! " he panted. " I lost touch with you and — "

" The battle ! " croaked Artor, interrupting him. " What's happening ? "

" It's as good as over, my lord. There's still some skirmishing going on beyond the hindmost ship, but most of the savages are running for their lives along the pass with a hundred warriors after them in full pursuit. I need but a couple of hours to clear up the mess and repair the damage, and then we can be on our way once more . . . But what of you, my lord ? And what miscreant bruised your neck ? "

Artor told him in as few words as possible, and then explained how Polda had saved his life.

" Orontes, you must do me a favour," he whispered. " I want you to give me Polda, so that I can thank him by setting him free."

" He's not mine to give, my lord," laughed Orontes. " He belongs to the men of Knossos, and is therefore as much yours as mine."

He turned to Polda and said, speaking slowly so that the man would understand : " Polda, from this moment henceforth you are in the personal service of the Lord Artor."

Polda's face lit up, and he said : " You mean, Lord Orontes, that never again shall I have to put my weight to the oar ? "

" Not unless the Lord Artor wills it," said Orontes. " You're his slave, now."

" Say, rather, my henchman," croaked Artor, still rubbing his throat. " In Sarm there are no slaves, and in Sarm the humblest peasant has as much right to live as the Pendragon himself."

# Chapter Thirteen

ALAYNE spent long hours at the window of her room watching the workmen clear up the damage caused by the earthquake. An entire wing of the Palace had collapsed, giving her a wider view of the city than before, and beyond the Palace she could see whole streets of shops and houses that had been reduced to rubble.

Little by little the people were returning to the city from the countryside where they had taken refuge, and it was heart-breaking to watch them picking over the ruins of their homes to salvage furniture and utensils.

Alayne's personal reaction to the earthquake was an increased respect for the people of Knossos — not only for their stoicism in the face of disaster, but also for their beliefs and teachings. She hadn't believed what she was told about the Earth-shaker, but now she realised it was nothing but the truth. So it was a greatly chastened Alayne who returned to the girls' suite from the Labyrinth, and when Raidne bade her make her peace with the King and drink the sacred wine, she obeyed without question.

She had been reprieved, but not forgiven, and now she was not allowed to mix with the other girls and no one spoke to her except Raidne and her tutors. Her meals were brought to her in her room, and she was constantly attended by slave-girls, whose function, it seemed, was as much to guard her as to serve. At the same time they stood in awe of her, glancing at her askance as they might at one who had returned from the dead. Whenever she tried to speak to them their only answer was to drop a scared curtsey and look away.

By night, one or another of them shared her room, sleeping in a truckle-bed placed across the doorway, and whenever Alayne asked Raidne how long she was to remain a prisoner, her question went unanswered.

For the rest, her life was much as it had been before she was taken to the Labyrinth. She was given lessons by the same tutors as before — the only difference being that she took the lessons alone — and the only time she even saw the other girls was during the sessions in the gymnasium. She guessed she wouldn't have seen them then except that most of the exercises needed the co-operation of two, three, four or more people, and the only words spoken to her were occasional friendly whispers when the instructress was looking the other way.

Now all the exercises involved bull-dancing, and presently the dummy bull was replaced by a live heifer with artificial horns strapped to its head, and at first Alayne was the only one of the girls who was not frightened of the little animal.

To bolster her self-respect she worked hard at excelling in all the exercises, and quite often, although she was supposed to be in disgrace, the instructress employed her to demonstrate difficult feats to the other girls.

Something happened during one of these sessions that filled her with excitement and anxiety about equal parts. The girls were learning to do the double leap-frog over the heifer's head and along its back and Alayne was deputed to steady each girl as she left the beast and landed on the safety-mattress. Daphne was particularly graceful at this manoeuvre, rarely needing Alayne's help at all, and so Alayne was extremely surprised when on Daphne's fourth or fifth attempt, she made a complete botch of it, missed out the second leap-frog altogether and rolled inelegantly over the animal's haunch.

Alayne darted forward to catch her, the heifer wheeled round and knocked them both over, and during that brief moment while they clung to each other, Daphne whispered : " Tonight . . . Don't sleep ! "

That was all, and the words were hardly spoken before the instructress was standing over them, upbraiding Daphne for her clumsiness and telling Alayne to get back to the mattress.

Alayne could guess that Daphne planned to come to her room that night and clearly she didn't know she was guarded, so she would be caught, and then what would happen to her ?

Alayne dreaded thinking about it, but had no chance to warn her friend before the session came to an end . . .

That evening seemed to last an eternity. She was longing to have a talk with Daphne, particularly now that she could speak the language of Knossos quite fluently, but she simply didn't see it happening. The slave-girl who would be on duty that night was a light sleeper and if Daphne woke her up she would be too scared not to report the matter to Raidne. Alayne had no illusions about her reputation. To the slave-girls she was practically a witch, someone who had spent ten days in the Labyrinth and then had emerged looking as if she'd hardly missed a meal. To Raidne she was a dangerous rebel, intent upon inciting all the girls to mutiny.

Meanwhile, the mere idea that she might talk to Daphne once more so heightened Alayne's curiosity that she felt she'd go mad if she didn't soon learn the answers to some of the questions that plagued her. First and foremost, why were they all there ? And why was so much importance attached to them ? And why did they have to learn so much ? And what was the significance of those rather absurd bull-dancing exercises ? And why, merely because she had refused to drink some wine, had she been imprisoned in the Labyrinth ? And then why had Raidne rescued her ? And above all, who was the young man who had brought her food ?

At last, the slave-girl who had been sitting with Alayne was joined by the one who would be sleeping there. Then Alayne's tension became almost unbearable. Would Daphne be sent to the Labyrinth ? Unlikely, she thought, but no doubt Raidne had other punishments up her sleeves that were nearly as horrible.

She wished the night were over, and could hardly contain her impatience at the time spent by the slave-girls in washing her hands and face and combing her hair.

It was odd that the girl on the night-duty seemed unusually sleepy. Two or three times she stifled yawns and, as soon as her colleague left, she dragged out the truckle-bed, undressed and slipped between the blankets.

This was unheard of. Other nights she sat on the bed for hours, embroidering by rush-light, or mending her clothes.

Lamplight flickered beyond the open door as Raidne made her rounds. As usual she ignored Alayne, and as usual Alayne stuck out her tongue as the older woman sailed past on her way to the staircase. And at the same moment she was struck by how regular was the breathing of her room-mate. She was asleep! It seemed impossible until Alayne remembered how she herself had been drugged by Sarpedon's men, and hit upon the probable explanation. Somehow or other Daphne had managed to get hold of a drug, and somehow or other she had administered it to the slave-girl.

There was no moon that night, and once the last vestiges of daylight had faded, Alayne had no means of gauging the passage of time at all.

To make quite sure she wouldn't fall asleep she got out of bed, put on her dressing-gown and went to the window, leaning on the sill as she gazed out over the stricken city. Here and there gangs of slaves were working by the light of blazing torches clearing up the debris, and on the city's outskirts she could see the camp-fires of the homeless who were now living the lives of outcasts in makeshift tents and shacks.

Farther away still, the great lantern of the Pharos — the lighthouse — glowed against the dark sky like a miniature moon. Below it, she could just make out the lights of ships riding at anchor in the harbour. In fact, she found the scene so absorbing that she almost jumped out of her skin when presently she heard someone whisper her name in the darkness.

She swung round, and gazed towards the door with her heart thumping wildly. The slave-girl was sound asleep, almost snoring, and Alayne could just discern Daphne's slender form as she edged her way past the truckle-bed.

" Over here, Daphne! I'm by the window and wide awake! "

After so many days of loneliness it was wonderful to have someone to talk to and, as Daphne pressed her hand, Alayne came uncomfortably close to tears.

" So the hemlock worked all right! " whispered Daphne,

as they sat down on the bed. " That girl won't open her eyes before morning."

" Hemlock ! " gasped Alayne. " But that's a deadly poison ! "

" Oh, we didn't give her much, and Lycastus's brother, who mixed the draught, swears it won't harm her. He's a trained apothecary." Daphne laughed softly, then added : " Guess how we got her to take it."

" I can't ! "

" We told her that her nose was getting bigger every day, and that there was only one medicine that could cure it . . . So when she wakes up in the morning be sure to tell her that her nose is smaller ! "

" All right ! " said Alayne, also laughing. " And who's Lycastus ? "

" Don't be silly," said Daphne. " You've better reason for knowing Lycastus than anyone. He's a bit soppy actually, but very useful . . . "

" But who is he ? "

" Why, the fellow who brought you food in the Labyrinth," said Daphne, in surprise. " Didn't he even tell you his name ? "

" No. I think he was too scared I might escape. He just pushed the basket through the door then locked me in again."

" He's in love with me," said Daphne, smugly, and explained that he was a member of the Palace guard.

" He must be a very brave young man."

" Oh, I don't know. All the guards are the same — they've only to win a smile from one of the bull-maidens to think they're made for life. They're such a superstitious lot ! "

" But how can you ever speak to him ? "

" Oh, he climbs up the creeper outside my room, and if he reaches up and I reach down we can just touch fingers. He's probably there now, poor dear ! "

This was news indeed. To have an ally on the outside — and a male ally bearing arms at that — put a different complexion on things, and Alayne was just as anxious to hear all about Lycastus as Daphne was to hear all about her experiences in the Labyrinth.

"Tell me," she whispered, "did you see the Minotaur?"

"I didn't see anyone or anything," Alayne told her. "It was as dark as the darkest night. I had to feel my way about by touch. Anyway, what is the Minotaur?"

"A terrible monster," said Daphne, shuddering. "Some say he's the same as the Earth-shaker, and others say that he's half bull and half man and that he devours people."

"Well, I didn't see him, and I'm glad I didn't hear about him until now."

Alayne wasn't allowed to change the subject until she had given Daphne a minute account of her life in the Labyrinth, but at least she learned why Raidne had rescued her.

"Raidne is a very frightened woman," said Daphne. "Here we are, with the Winter Festival only three months away, and we're still below strength. There should be at least seven bull-maidens and there are only six of us. They say that one girl jumped from the White Ship and got away in the ship's boat."

"I know," said Alayne. "I saw her do it. But go on . . ."

" Most years there are more than enough girls, and some are held over till the following year, but now it seems that all the nations are defying Knossos, and are hiding their well-born youths and maidens — "

" Youths as well ? "

" Yes, of course — the ordinances of the Festival demand seven youths and seven maidens. Really, Alayne my sweet — don't they tell you anything in your part of the world ? "

" Not much," agreed Alayne, with a laugh. " But finish telling me about Raidne."

" Well, when you defied her," said Daphne, " she began to fear that we'd all mutiny and so had to make an example of you. Then there were only five bull-maidens left, but she wasn't too worried because the White Ship was expected to put in at about that time and she thought that she could count on it bringing at least two more girls, including the one who had escaped before. Then came terrible news — the White Ship had been driven on to some rocks by a storm, and had foundered with all hands."

Alayne gave a gasp of horror. " Was Thara on board her ? " she asked.

" Thara ? "

" She was the girl who got away in the ship's boat. Was she drowned ? "

" I don't know," said Daphne. " Lycastus couldn't give me many details, but I know that the fishing-boat that brought the news wasn't able to pick up any survivors."

" I can't think that Thara was on board," murmured Alayne. " She would never let herself be captured a second time. And now there's no White Ship ? "

" Oh, yes, there is," said Daphne. " One of the war galleys was commissioned to replace her, and is away at this moment searching for well-born maidens. Oh, it was terrible here when we heard about the loss of the other ship. The Court proclaimed a day of mourning, we had to fast from dawn to dusk, and they say that more than a hundred bulls were sacrificed to appease the gods. It should have been a thousand I think, because the next thing that happened was the earthquake, and then Raidne must have wondered whether she caused all the disasters by imprisoning you in the Labyrinth. All we know is that while the earth was still rumbling, and before the last of the buildings had crashed to the ground, she went to the Temple of the Snake Goddess and consulted the High Priestess, and the following day you were back."

Alayne was silent for some minutes, piecing together the sequence of events and trying to make out what made the people of Knossos behave as they behaved.

Finally she said : " Daphne, do you really believe all this business about the bulls ? "

" What else can one believe ? " asked Daphne. " All power stems from the bulls and one can see it in the simplest things. Would our cornfields flourish as they do were it not for the bulls dragging the ploughs over them ? And what is ploughing but a means of transmitting the bull's strength into the soil ? Remember, Alayne, you laughed when I told you about the Earth-shaker, but I don't think you'd be so ready to laugh now."

" No, I certainly shouldn't," agreed Alayne, " but I still find it all rather hard to understand. Anyway, why are *we* here ? And what part do we play in the Winter Festival ? "

She heard Daphne give a little gasp, and it seemed that for some moments the other girl was too startled to speak.

" Do you really mean to tell me you don't know ? " she said, eventually.

" I know no more than I've guessed," Alayne assured her, " and that's not much."

Her position was quite different from that of the other girls. They all of them came from lands bordering the inland sea, and most of them had been brought up to believe in the cult of the bulls. Alayne was the first girl to be captured by ships of the northern route, and that she had been taken at all showed what desperate straits the men of Knossos were in. Why, she wasn't even very well born by their standards !

Daphne stirred uneasily, making the bed rustle. " Then I don't know that I should tell you," she whispered. " That's a job for Raidne, or one of the Priestesses."

" Raidne hardly speaks to me," said Alayne. " Oh, come on Daphne — we're friends, aren't we ? "

" All right — as long as you promise never to tell anyone I told you."

" I promise."

It seemed that the great Winter Festival was what Knossos lived by — unless it was celebrated annually every one of its inhabitants, from King Minos down to the scruffiest slave, believed that the city would perish and its citizens die. It went on for six days, of which the first three were given over to feasting and rejoicing, and the last three to the sinister observances of the cult.

" First the citizens celebrate the successful ending of another year," said Daphne, " and then they prepare for the year to come." She hesitated, then added sombrely : " And the fourth day is our day."

" Well, go on — explain."

" Each year a supreme bull is chosen from all the hundreds that are brought to Knossos," said Daphne, " and of course this year Leucoperses is the ruling bull. We shall encounter him on the fourth day of the Festival, and then the following day it will be the turn of the youths, and on the sixth and last day he is sacrificed by the hand of King Minos himself."

" We encounter him ? " queried Alayne. " What does that mean ? "

" We meet him in the secret arena of the Palace, and then we dance the age-old Dance of the Ruling Bull, the figures of which we are now being taught — "

" But he will attack us ! " put in Alayne.

" Naturally, and it behoves us to evade him until we can do so no longer. Then, as one by one we die, Leucoperses will assimilate all our virtues, breeding, beauty and learning, just as on the following day he will acquire the corresponding qualities of the youths. On the final day Leucoperses dies that Knossos may live."

Alayne could hardly believe her ears, and the thing that

astonished her most was the way in which Daphne — and all the girls for that matter — took it so calmly.

" But aren't you terrified ? " she asked, saying the first thing that came into her head.

" A little," agreed Daphne. " But on the whole I am too conscious of the great honour of being a bull-maiden to feel really frightened."

" But we're all so young ! " cried Alayne, exasperated. " Oh, Daphne, how can you take it so calmly ? "

" Because the price we pay is so small," said Daphne, " and the reward is so great. The end may be painful — agonising, even — and then we go at once to dwell with the gods and goddesses in Elysium, and there we shall live for ever, always young, always beautiful, and eternally beyond the reach of pain or misery."

" H'm ! I wish I felt so confident," muttered Alayne, then caught her breath sharply as Daphne touched her arm and whispered : " Listen ! "

Someone was moving. They heard the patter of bare feet along the corridor, and then a girl's voice shouting Raidne's name at the top of the stairs.

" It's Arisbe ! " breathed Daphne, mentioning the name of one of the two girls from Troy. " Get into bed, Alayne ! "

" But what about you ? " whispered Alayne, as she slipped out of her dressing-gown. " You'd better get back to your own room."

" No," said Daphne, " it's safer here. Arisbe's at the top of the stairs and I'd have to pass her."

Alayne climbed into bed, hardly daring to breathe. The lamp-light flickered palely beyond the doorway and then came Raidne's voice asking Arisbe what was the matter.

" It's Daphne ! " they heard Arisbe reply. " She's not in her room . . . I've got a cold and went to her to borrow some hand-kerchiefs . . . "

Daphne went to the door, deciding to brazen it out. " It's all right, Raidne," she called. " I'm here — in Alayne's room."

" You're where ? " cried Raidne, almost screaming. " You're

in Alayne's room ? "

" That's right," said Daphne, calmly, and Alayne, out of the corner of her eye, saw the rays from the lamp wheel across the ceiling. " She woke me up screaming and groaning and I came to see what was the matter. I thought she was being ill but she seems quite all right. I suppose it was a nightmare."

" But you know quite well you're forbidden to speak to her — "

" I didn't speak to her, Raidne," said Daphne, mildly. " Anyway, I think she's still half asleep."

" Well, get back to your rooms, both of you," snapped Raidne, and as Daphne and Arisbe padded away along the corridor Alayne guessed that Raidne was gazing down at the slave-girl, wondering why she hadn't wakened. To distract her, Alayne essayed a little moan and turned over in bed.

" It's the Earth-shaker," she mumbled. " The Earth-shaker . . . help me ! "

Raidne came quickly to the bed and leant over her. " Alayne . . . what's the matter ? "

Alayne turned on to her back and blinked up at her, screwing up her eyes against the light.

" What's wrong ? " she murmured sleepily.

" Nothing, dear. You were dreaming . . . Here, drink some water."

Alayne sat up in bed and let Raidne hold the little goblet to her lips.

" Thank you, Raidne . . . Oh, it's wonderful to know it was only a dream ! "

" You had a nightmare, had you ? "

" I suppose you'd call it that, but it wasn't so bad as some. I have bad dreams nearly every night now. I dreamt I was back in the Labyrinth, and you were mixed up in it somehow . . . Oh, yes, you'd been sent down there because we're a girl short."

Alayne heard the older woman catch her breath and grinned inwardly. Raidne was quite clearly unnerved, and the hand holding the lamp trembled visibly, making the shadows dance. Then she sat down on the bed and stroked Alayne's hair.

" Listen, my dear — if I let you mix with the other girls as before, will you promise you won't try to subvert them ? "

" What does ' subvert ' mean ? "

" You won't be disobedient or rebellious, or persuade them to be ? "

" But I couldn't ! " said Alayne, virtuously, yet not promising. " They're all far too proud of being chosen as bull-maidens. They wouldn't listen to me."

" All right, Alayne. Your punishment's over, and tomorrow you can join the other girls."

It was an improvement, certainly, but Alayne still had a great deal to worry about. Now the overriding problem was how to escape from Knossos before the Winter Festival came round.

# Chapter Fourteen

SUMMER was well advanced before Artor reached the great island where Zagreus, the commander of the planned expedition against Knossos, had his headquarters.

The four ships, shaken by their rough journey across the mountains, then damaged in the battle, took longer to repair than had been expected, but at least the artisans had been able to make all four seaworthy once more. Then Artor had the good luck to have perfect weather for his voyage to the island where the little fleet now lay.

King Kancho voyaged with him as his guest, and to introduce him to Zagreus.

Artor was so used to commanders being burly, boisterous men that Zagreus came almost as a shock to him. He was so tiny as to be almost a dwarf, and although he was only in his forties his face was deeply furrowed and his pale hair was going thin on top ; and so far from being fond of the sound of his own voice, he seemed to spend most of his time listening to those about him.

His headquarters, too, were unpretentious. He himself dwelt and held conferences in a large tent, and his followers either lived on board ship or in the island's numerous caves.

So that no wind of the enterprise should reach Knossos the ships were dispersed among the coves and inlets with which the island's coast was fretted.

Zagreus spoke no language but Greek, which meant that Orontes had to act as interpreter between him and Artor, and Artor's first impressions were far from favourable.

He told Orontes so, saying : " I'm in extremely low spirits, Orontes. As I see it we have come these great distances, and braved those many perils only to discover that there's no real hope of rescuing Alayne."

" Why do you say that, my lord ? "

" Because of the whole attitude of this strange, little man," said Artor, hotly. " He seems to have no sense of urgency. Didn't he say more than once that our greatest mistake would be to launch an attack before we were ready ? "

" Well, my lord, it would be hard to think of a greater," smiled Orontes. " I must admit that my impression of him was quite different from yours, my lord. But then, I had the advantage of speaking to him in his native language. He impressed me as having a greater brain than any man I've ever met."

" But, Orontes, even the greatest brain can't win battles with insufficient ships and warriors. Before I came here I expected to see great fleets of ships lying at anchor, and I thought the shores of this island would be teeming with warriors."

" My lord, sometimes a commander is wise not to reveal his full strength even to his allies. We know that King Kancho has a large fleet of ships, as well as numerous warriors. They are not here, but they could be summoned hither within a matter of days, and I believe that Zagreus is in touch with a dozen such rulers."

" Even so," said Artor, glumly, " I don't see us getting to Knossos before the Winter Festival, and you yourself said that Alayne had little chance of surviving that. Zagreus spoke of an invasion next year, or even the year after."

" My lord, may I refresh your memory ? " asked Orontes. " In fact, Zagreus said that until a few months ago he hadn't considered the possibility of an invasion for a year or even two, but since then a number of things have happened. First, there was the sun's eclipse. He himself does not attach great importance to it, but he knows that it must have disturbed the men of Knossos, and he knows that it has put great heart into their enemies. Then there was the loss of the White Ship — as great a blow as if Zeus himself had struck King Minos's face. And before Knossos had recovered from it, a third of the city was laid low by the earthquake. To those considerations we now add another, by bringing Zagreus four ships that can sail into the enemy harbour at any time without question."

" Then why does Zagreus hesitate ? " asked Artor. " If I

were in his position I'd start to deploy my forces right away."

" No doubt," said Orontes, dryly. " But Zagreus is a cautious man, and we must allow him the few days' grace he has asked for. He needs to think things over, and I am confident that when he gives us his answer it will be a positive one with no nonsense about it."

So Artor was left with no choice but to contain his impatience for a little longer, and he spent the following three days mostly in Polda's company, listening to the former slave's tales of the strange countries he had visited, and exploring the nearer parts of the island with him.

Artor found the island's native population oddly interesting, since in their behaviour they were quite different from the people of any other land he had visited, but he wasn't able to make any contact with them. Small, dark people for the most part, they were aloof and timid, but they were certainly not savages, for they lived in small round houses built of stone with such skill that one could imagine them lasting just as long as Sarm's great Stone Circle would last.

Where these people differed from most was in their peace-fulness. They appeared to have no warriors or fighting men, and little use for bows and arrows, for they were not given to hunting, and lived mainly on fish, fruit and vegetables and the milk produced by their large herds of goats.

The sullen glances they threw Artor and Polda were proof of the resentment they felt at having the strangers on their island, but this resentment was tempered a great deal by Zagreus's sensible handling of the problem. He restrained fire-eating warriors such as King Kancho from raiding the native settlements, and even insisted on paying the natives rent in the form of linen and dressed skins. The warriors thought he was mad but they also realised that his was the sort of madness that could gain them victory over Knossos.

When the three days had gone by and Artor was again sum-moned to Zagreus's tent he received something of a shock as soon as he entered it.

At his first interview with the commander there had been

no one present except Orontes, but now Zagreus was attended by three other people, and two of them looked so fierce and barbaric that Artor had to restrain his first impulse, which was to draw his dagger. They were a man and a girl and there was enough likeness between them to suggest they might be father and daughter for they both had black curling hair and flashing eyes, and both looked as fearless as the bravest of warriors. The man was imposing enough, but it was the girl who most impresssed Artor — he had rarely seen anyone so beautiful and it was hard to believe that she was a human being and not a goddess.

The third member of the group was a quite insignificant old man, whose function, Artor learned presently, was to act as interpreter between Zagreus and the other two.

Zagreus greeted Artor formally and then made a speech which was, for him, quite wordy.

He said, according to Orontes's translation : " Greetings, Lord Artor, visitor from distant Sarm ! May I introduce you to my other two guests — the Prince-Paramount Laikul, and his daughter the Princess Thara. Prince Laikul rules great areas of a large island some distance to the south-east of this one, and I'm sure you will have a particular interest in meeting his daughter since she is well known to your cousin, the Lady Alayne . . . "

Artor interrupted at this point, thinking that Orontes had misinterpreted. After all, he knew everyone that Alayne knew, and he was certain that no Princess Thara had ever visited Dort or Sarm.

However, Orontes insisted that he hadn't made a mistake, and then, with growing excitement, Artor learned of the friendship that had sprung up between Alayne and Thara on board the White Ship.

Thara's ruse by which she had escaped from the ship thrilled him until he had time to think about it, and then he threw Orontes an anxious glance.

" But the Princess says she doesn't know quite what happened to Alayne," he pointed out, " so how do we know she wasn't killed by the bull ? "

Orontes smiled reassuringly, and told him that Alayne was certainly on board the White Ship when it reached Knossos.

" As you know, my lord, we have many friends among the seamen of Knossos," he said, " and from them we know that the ship returned to harbour under white sails. If there had not been a bull-maiden on board the sails would have been black."

" There is no room for any doubt ? "

" None at all, my lord. The Lady Alayne is certainly in Knossos at this moment."

In all it had taken Thara about a month to get home after escaping from the ship. The natives of the first island she had landed on would have nothing to do with her, believing her to be a sea-witch, but at the next island she was luckier, and she succeeded in convincing its inhabitants that she was a princess whose father would reward them richly if they took her to him. This they agreed to do, but as their only vessels were small fishing-boats the voyage had been long and tedious in the extreme.

" Ever since her escape," said Orontes, interpreting Zagreus, " the men of Knossos have given her father no peace. In spite of all his protests they suspect that he is hiding her and have threatened him with full-scale war unless he gives her up. In the end they had to flee, and after numerous adventures reached this island some twenty days ago."

Artor could guess that Zagreus had not summoned him merely to hear an account of Thara's experiences, and he was gratified, although not surprised, when the commander informed him, through Orontes, that a date for the invasion had been fixed.

" And it is to coincide with this year's Winter Festival, my lord," said Orontes, then went on to explain that the festival lasted six days, of which the fourth was the fatal one from the point of view of the bull-maidens.

Orontes said : " Therefore, my lord, the commander has decided to strike on the third day, when the rejoicings will be at their height and when there will hardly be a sober man in the whole city. As you are aware, our cause has numerous sympathisers in Knossos — even within the Palace itself — but communication with them always presents difficulties. Yet there are enough of them to create a major disturbance in support of the invasion if only they knew its exact date, and it is in that connection that the Princess Thara has most courageously agreed to help. She and her father intend to return to their own land forthwith, whereupon the Princess will allow herself to be recaptured by the men of Knossos. The commander's most influential agent in Knossos actually lives within the walls of the Palace itself, and it is to him that Thara will take a message. He is an elderly Athenian, a painter by profession, and he has the duty of teaching the bull-maidens the elements of drawing and painting — "

" Why ? " asked Artor.

" My lord, the bull-maidens learn many crafts and skills, that they may be passed on to the bull at the time of their — their . . . "

He broke off in some confusion, and Artor, knowing that it was almost blasphemy for the shipmaster to speak of these matters, did not press him, and said, instead : " But how can the Princess convey a message ? I gather that she speaks no language but her own ? "

" That is so, my lord, but both the Athenian and the commander are experts in this strange skill known as ' writing '. The commander will make certain black marks on a piece of leather, and this leather the Princess will give to the Athenian. The marks on it will tell him exactly what is planned."

" Do you think it will work ? " asked Artor, doubtfully.

" I am certain of it, my lord. Why, there are men in the harbour offices at Knossos who can consult clay tablets and give you the exact details of cargoes carried even years before, together with the names of the ports they were carried from and to. The marks on the tablets never forget or make a mistake."

" It takes some believing ! " said Artor, smiling good-humouredly. " Still, be that as it may, we've gained our main point, and we shall rescue the Lady Alayne before the Winter Festival ! "

" Yes, my lord. That is, as long as we're not defeated."

" Oh, we shan't be ! " said Artor, cheerfully, and then an

exciting idea occurred to him — he could send a message to Alayne by teaching it to the Princess Thara word by word, and he asked Orontes what he thought of the idea.

" It should work, my lord," said the shipmaster. " The Princess may have the temper of a wild cat, but she looks highly intelligent and we know that she's well-disposed towards us. I will talk to her interpreter about it."

He did so, and the outcome of it was that Thara spent what little time remained to her before she left for her own land in the company of Artor and the two interpreters.

Artor's message to Alayne, composed with Orontes's help, was a long one, but Thara had no difficulty in learning it and she was still word-perfect the following morning when she stepped aboard the little fishing vessel that was to take her and her father to their homeland.

Artor was impressed by the dignity of her departure, for she faced the future with its unknown hazards as calmly and as fearlessly as a seasoned warrior, and the Prince Laikul made a short speech of farewell to the assembled company, in which he said that though he had few warriors and no ships, he at least had a daughter who would play her part in the struggle against Knossos as unflinchingly as the bravest fighting man ever born.

" We have suffered too long the insults of these arrogant tyrants," he concluded, " and now Knossos must fall ! "

# Chapter Fifteen

THE days were shortening noticeably, and soon it would be autumn. A feverishness had entered into the training of the bull-maidens, and now more than half the daylight hours were spent in teaching them the Dance of the Ruling Bull, and the intensity was such that Alayne found it hard not to accept the beliefs of those about her, even half-believing Daphne when she insisted that an hour or so's agony would be exchanged for an eternity of perfect happiness.

Then, suddenly, the whole picture changed and one morning Alayne was awakened by such a clamour of trumpets and bells that her first thought was that the whole population of Knossos had gone mad with joy. As long as she lived she would never forget the excitements of that day.

Even while the bells were still ringing and the trumpets still blaring, Raidne called all the girls together and told them that they were to have a full day's holiday, culminating in the most sumptuous banquet that the Palace's larders could provide. Moreover, they were all to be given new dresses and then they would be borne in litters to the harbour, because, she explained, the White Ship had put in during the night and on board her was the seventh bull-maiden.

" What is more," went on Raidne, " she is the same Princess who earlier this year escaped from the White Ship, and thus brought about the darkening of the sun that has boded so ill for our great city . . . "

Thara ! Alayne joined her cheers to those of the others, but whereas they were rejoicing in the arrival of the seventh bull-maiden she was rejoicing in the knowledge that soon she would have an ally, and one brave enough to defy even the Earth-shaker himself if he stood in her way.

The only puzzling thing about it was how Thara had ever

come to be recaptured, and Alayne could guess that it had taken a whole army to do it.

"The city rejoices," said Raidne, "and later the priests and priestesses of all the temples will join together in giving thanks to the gods for this sign of our return to favour. Especially, they will ask the gods' permission to wipe the day of the sun's eclipse from our calendars and to expunge it from our records as if it had never existed . . . "

A little later, as Alayne was getting ready for the journey to the harbour, Raidne came to her room and told her that on the return journey she would share a litter with the Princess Thara.

"You see, Alayne, you already know her," she said, "and it will cheer her up to be met by a familiar face. Do you speak the same language ? "

"No," said Alayne, "but we can usually make each other understand."

"Good ! Because clearly the Princess has a rebellious nature, and so, once, had you. However, you've learnt that rebellion doesn't pay, and perhaps you'll be able to pass the knowledge on to the Princess."

"Perhaps ! " agreed Alayne, and smiled, reflecting that Raidne had no idea of what she was up against. She remembered how Thara had behaved on the occasion of her first capture, and found it hard not to laugh aloud when Raidne went on to speak of the newcomer's education.

"She'll have to work very hard," she said, "if she's to learn even the least that a bull-maiden must learn before her great day. Would you say she's quick-witted ? "

"Extremely ! " said Alayne, and wondered if Raidne would have looked so happy had she realised just what forms Thara's intelligence took . . .

With the exception of King Minos and his Queen, the whole Palace turned out to greet the seventh bull-maiden, and the procession was headed by Leucoperses whom Alayne had not seen since her early days in Knossos.

He looked larger than ever, and Alayne could hardly believe

that once, clinging to those great horns, she had rendered him powerless. Also, and this was for the first time, she saw the seven male bull-dancers. They marched beside the litters in which the girls rode, and Alayne scanned their faces eagerly in the hope of finding potential allies, but she was disappointed. All the youths, gazing directly ahead, had the look of dedicated men, and as she studied those bronzed and handsome faces she guessed that their indoctrination had been even more thorough-going than the girls.

In fact, wherever she looked, she found the same qualities — in everyone's face was the same fanatical belief in the omnipotence of the bull, and if there were any doubters in Knossos she could only suppose that they had not joined the procession.

Her greatest surprise of the day came when she first set eyes on Thara. She wouldn't have been altogether astonished to find the girl bound hand and foot — or even locked in a cage like a wild animal — but to see her serene and smiling and beautifully dressed in white linen was a tremendous shock.

She was standing on the deck of the White Ship when Alayne first saw her, flanked by two gaunt-faced priestesses, and to all appearances she looked perfectly happy and composed, so much so that Alayne's heart sank and she wondered if by some magic the men of Knossos had succeeded in breaking the Princess's spirit and reducing her to the same state of abject acquiescence in their beliefs as affected the other girls.

It was a day of brilliant sunshine, but for Alayne the skies seemed to darken at that moment, and as she gazed at Thara, so smiling and complacent, her last hope of an ally vanished like smoke.

The reception formalities were prolonged and tedious, and for Alayne the day did not become real again until she saw Raidne, accompanied by the two priestesses, escorting Thara towards her litter. Then, as Raidne reintroduced the two girls, Thara flashed Alayne the briefest of winks, and in that instant Alayne realised that her friend was there, not because the men of Knossos willed it, but because she, Thara, willed it.

Her spirits soared wildly, and before she had time to collect her thoughts, Thara was in the litter at her side, and the procession had started on its way back to the city.

Thara pressed her hand, and as soon as the cheers had died a little, whispered : " Alayne, I have a message — "

Alayne gazed at her in astonishment. " Thara, you're speaking the language of Sarm ! " she exclaimed, but the other girl merely looked a little confused, and repeated : " Alayne, I have a message for you from the Lord Artor — "

Again Alayne, almost beside herself with excitement, interrupted her : " From Artor ? But where is he ? " And then, when she saw no response in Thara's face, it dawned upon her that Thara was repeating a message that she had learnt by heart.

Thara tried again. " Alayne, I have a message for you from the Lord Artor," she said. " You must be of good heart for really great help is on the way. All being well it will arrive on the third day of the Winter Festival. It will be supported by groups of sympathisers living in the city of Knossos itself, and at the height of the festivities they will launch an attack upon the Palace to coincide with the landing of the invading forces on the beaches. When the attack is launched make every effort to escape from the Palace in the confusion and if successful, head for the harbour. Beneath the first flight of stairs leading up to the Pharos there is a store-room where the lamp-oil and candles are kept. Hide in there and you will be rescued as soon as the fighting is over."

" But — " began Alayne, then realised that it was no use asking Thara questions. All the questions that tumbled into her mind would have to remain unanswered until she saw Artor. It all seemed as magical as if the Great Warrior himself had addressed her from the clouds.

How had Artor managed to reach the inland sea? And how had he come into contact with Thara? And how came he to know so much about Knossos that he could even say where the lighthouse men kept their oil and candles? Surely that must mean that he had the shipmaster, Orontes, on his side, and together they must be in possession of at least one of the great ships of Knossos.

The whole aspect of things had changed so abruptly and unexpectedly that she knew it would be hours before she had really taken it in, and meanwhile she was so happy that she could have sung at the top of her voice all the way back to the city . . .

The days that followed were enchanted ones. Thara was given the room next to hers, and no one thought it odd that they should spend almost all their free time together. Raidne was convinced that Alayne was acting as a good influence upon Thara, and in any case Thara was on such good behaviour that hardly anyone remembered that she had once escaped from the White Ship. Now that she was in the Palace she was obedient and industrious, and she worked extremely hard at her lessons. It was in her interests to do so, since the sooner she learned Greek, the sooner had she and Alayne a language in common, and in fact, before she had been in Knossos a month she and Alayne could converse almost as easily as if they were sisters . . .

Soon only a few handfuls of days separated them from the Winter Festival, and then came a morning when the little old art master kept Alayne back after the rest of the class, ostensibly to talk about one of her drawings.

Thara had told Alayne that the art master was an enemy of King Minos and on their side, but he had never shown any sign of it until now when, as he criticised her drawing, she heard him say without the slightest change of tone : " The signal for the rising will be three short blasts on a whistle and it will be repeated several times as the section-leaders rally their followers. The password is ' The Lion Roars ' and it will enable you to get to the harbour should any of our followers stop you."

Then he went on discussing her drawings so blandly that it was hard not to think she had dreamt his other remarks.

" Does Thara know ? " she whispered, for Thara, as a novice, had her lessons apart from the other girls.

" She knows, and now you do understand what I mean about the contours ? Look after the contours and the drawing will look after itself."

" I understand," said Alayne, cheerfully, and as she went gaily back to her room had the greatest difficulty in not shouting " The Lion Roars " at the top of her voice. Actually neither she nor Thara had ever seen a lion, and only knew that it was something like a wild cat, but larger, and the idea of a cat roaring struck them both as wonderfully silly and amusing . . .

# Chapter Sixteen

ON the day when the seven bull-maidens were given their final fittings for the gorgeous gold-and-white costumes that they would wear for the Dance of the Ruling Bull an extraordinary thing happened.

A huge eagle, as white as a swan, was seen to approach Knossos from the north, and when it reached the city it circled the Palace three times and then came to rest on the tower of the Snake Goddess's temple, where it stayed until nightfall.

No one doubted that this was a good omen of the highest order, and long before the priests and priestesses had deliberated on the matter and given their verdict, the ordinary people of Knossos had made up their minds. They were certain that the eagle could be none other than the god Zeus himself. They poured out into the streets in such numbers that a stranger could be forgiven for supposing that the Festival had begun.

That evening Alayne and Thara watched the celebrations — the torchlight processions and the bonfires — from the roof-garden, and with the last of the daylight came a great fanfare of trumpets which temporarily reduced the crowds to silence.

"That's to announce the voice of the High Priest," said Alayne. "The same thing happened on the day of the sun's eclipse."

She had to repeat the words before Thara understood them, but this was unusual. The Princess had picked up the rudiments of Greek extraordinarily quickly, and on most subjects the two girls could converse as easily as if it were their native language. Thara hadn't shown a similar aptitude for the bull-dancing, which she thought stupid, but her mentors were too pleased at having found their seventh bull-maiden to be critical, and she herself expected to escape before the Dance of the Ruling Bull ever took place.

" Listen ! " murmured Alayne, and from the Snake Goddess's temple they could hear the High Priest's reedy voice speaking in the measured tones of one making a solemn proclamation.

" Can you hear what he says ? " asked Thara.

" No, but the Palace heralds will repeat it," said Alayne, and the words were hardly out of her mouth before they heard another fanfare to announce the King's herald, and then the sound of his voice as he roared the proclamation from the battlements. There was a long preamble to the announcement which was beyond Alayne's understanding, but the body of the message was straightforward enough, and she put it into simpler words for Thara's benefit.

" All it amounts to," she said, " is that the priests and priest-esses are quite sure that the white eagle was Zeus himself, and they say that the purpose of his visit was to tell the city its sins were forgiven now that the seventh bull-maiden had been secured. The gods have considered the city's plea to have the day of the sun's eclipse wiped from the calendar, and they have agreed to it wholeheartedly — "

The trumpets blared again and she broke off abruptly as the herald added something to his statement. What he said came as a terrible shock to her, and she caught hold of Thara's hand to steady herself.

" Did you get that, Thara ? " she gasped.

" Something about the Festival ? "

" Yes . . . Thara, this is awful ! "

" Well, what did he say ? "

" Why, that due to the shortening of the calendar, the dates of the Festival have all been brought forward by one day. You see what that means ? "

Thara thought for a moment, then gave a gasp of dismay.

" Why, yes — the Dance of the Ruling Bull will now take place on the day planned for the invasion ! "

" Exactly," agreed Alayne, sombrely. " And we'll be dead before the city is freed."

" But perhaps not," said Thara. " Perhaps the invaders will learn of the change in the calendar and alter their plans."

" How can they ? They must be at sea by now, on their way here."

The prospect was an appalling one, and at the first opportunity the girls talked the matter over with the art master, only to find him as disturbed as they were.

" I can offer you only the smallest grain of hope," he told them. " As soon as I heard of the alteration to the calendar I sent out a fishing-boat to meet the invading fleet, but the chances of an encounter are small, and in any case our friends may not be able to advance their plans by a whole day."

" Then we must escape before the Festival," said Alayne, but even as she spoke she knew it would be an impossibility. Now that the Festival was only a few days away, Raidne was taking no chances. The force guarding the bull-maidens' suite had been doubled, and the old guard had been relieved, so that any slight acquaintanceship that had sprung up between the soldiers and the girls could not be exploited.

By night Raidne paid numerous visits to the suite, accompanied by two or more of the toughest slave-women, and the lamps in the corridors were never put out. Even if the girls succeeded in getting out of the suite there would still be the problem of escaping from the Palace, and finally from the city itself with its great walls and massive gates.

As the remaining days passed it became increasingly hard for Alayne and Thara to talk things over. They were rehearsing the dance so intensively that they were almost never alone together, and now that perfecting the dance was all-important, they no longer saw anything of the art master.

On the very eve of the Festival they did manage to get a few minutes together in Thara's room, and held a hurried conference.

" If the invasion doesn't come on the third day," said Alayne, " our only hope is that it takes place early on the fourth. I gather that we're not taken to the arena until midday and then the bull isn't released upon us until the middle of the afternoon."

" It's a slender hope," remarked Thara. " The attack on the harbour and the beaches will probably be launched at dawn, but even if all goes well the advance to the city will take the better part of the day. Anyway, there's little we can do except trust to luck. But I'll make you this promise — I shan't escape without you."

" Nor I without you," agreed Alayne, and they were kissing hands on the bargain when Daphne came in, white-faced and excited.

" I feel half like a goddess," she told them, " and half as if I'm going to be sick at any moment. I simply don't know how I'll get through the next three days."

Her remark gave Alayne an idea, and she asked what would happen if a girl were taken ill before the great dance, but the reply was not helpful.

" It just doesn't happen," said Daphne. " From the moment we drink the Snake Goddess's wine we are as goddesses ourselves, and invulnerable to everything except the assaults of the Ruling Bull. You could throw yourself from the battlements to the courtyard without so much as breaking a finger-nail."

" I don't believe it," said Thara, but both she and Alayne could see that they would gain nothing by pretending to be ill. The authorities simply would not believe it possible, and they would be sent to the arena even if they had to be carried there on stretchers . . .

So the Festival dawned, and before the notes of the inaugural fanfare had died away, the city seemed to go mad.

Huge quantities of food and wine were made freely available to the populace, and the hours were packed with music and dancing as tightly as the streets were packed with people, but none of this much affected the bull-maidens. They carried on with the rehearsals, and now that they were considered invulnerable, they worked with an almost full-sized bull to represent Leucoperses.

When they weren't rehearsing they were taken from one temple to another to endure elaborate ceremonies of purification, and the only respite they had was in the evenings when they regaled with food and wine as exquisite as that served to King Minos himself.

Musicians and dancers performed for their enjoyment, and from the roof-garden they could see the multi-coloured flames of the bonfires piercing the darkness from the city to the coast.

Alayne and Thara drifted through the first two days as though in a dream, but from the moment of waking on the third day they were alert for any sign of the invasion. Throughout the day they kept as close to each other as they could, straining their ears for the sounds of battle, half-expecting at any moment to hear the three whistle blasts that would announce the rising, but the day closed just as the two that preceded it had closed, except that the sounds of revelry from the streets were wilder, the bonfires more numerous and the music louder.

That night, before they went to bed, they were attended by Raidne, their teachers and various of the slave-girls, all come to say their farewells, for they would awake the following morning as goddesses not to be addressed by mortals.

As the art master said his good-bye to Alayne he whispered : " All goes well ! " and although the phrase could mean little or nothing Alayne clutched it as a drowning man a straw and repeated it over and over to herself throughout that almost sleepless night . . .

It was a strange thing, but the next morning Alayne actually felt a little as if she had been translated to a more sacred state of being, but no doubt that was because the slave-girls who helped her bathe and dress went in such awe of her, never speaking to her and not even to each other above a whisper.

The preparations took hours, and all the while, as the girls dressed her hair, polished her nails and finally helped her into the elaborately flounced gold-and-white dress that was the traditional costume for the Dance of the Ruling Bull, Alayne listened for any sound that might suggest that an attack had been launched, but the great city was as silent as a graveyard, with a silence that sounded all the deeper in contrast to the noise of the previous three days.

The food that was brought to her room was delicious but she was too anxious to eat more than a few mouthfuls, and all too soon came the thunder of the drums summoning the bull-maidens to the arena.

Raidne led the way, and they moved in single file behind her, walking slowly, pausing at each step, and seeing no one on any of the staircases or in the corridors throughout the journey. Soon they were below ground-level and moving along passages lit by blazing torches, and Alayne caught glimpses of wonderful murals illustrating phases of the great dance. She guessed that they were in the vicinity of the Labyrinth, for the air had a faintly dank smell, and from the distance she could hear the lowing and stamping of cattle.

Tall bronze doors were thrown open and they found themselves in the vestibule of the arena dedicated to the Snake Goddess, and knew that only one pair of doors now divided them from the arena itself.

Seven priestesses came forward and went on their knees to them, then each handed the girl opposite her a large square of scarlet linen, which would be her only defence against Leuco-perses.

The High Priestess threw incense into a brazier, a gong sounded and then from the direction of the arena came an incantation sung by male voices.

Alayne, as the leading dancer, took up a position by the arena's doors and wished she had the moral courage to stage a protest, to overturn the brazier and slap the High Priestess's face, but as it was she was too much under the influence of the ritual even to dare catch Thara's eye and wink.

As she stood waiting for the second gong to sound she could not help feeling awed by the thought that within moments she would find herself facing King Minos in all his glory.

The singing of the priestly choir grew stronger, soared upwards to a climax and then the gong was struck, filling Alayne with a sense of foreboding that turned all her muscles to water.

The great doors opened, plunging Alayne into a blaze of light so dazzling that she could see nothing except the golden pole that marked the arena's centre. Towards this she advanced with three girls on each side of her and a pace behind, and as she reached the pole the ritual music started, familiar because she had been rehearsing to it for weeks, yet unfamiliar because now it was played by some fifty instruments instead of only one.

As she tripped her way mechanically through the Dance's elaborate figures, she began to take in more of her surroundings, the rows upon rows of priests and priestesses, assignable to

their various orders by the colours of their sashes, the black-clad choir and the blue-garbed orchestra, plucking their lyres and beating their drums in the space allotted to them immediately below the Royal recess.

Then, as she grew more sure of herself and more confident that she was dancing well, she lifted her eyes and gazed upon the King himself, a lonely gilded figure enthroned somewhat ahead of his Queen, but yet looking no more remarkable than ten thousand other men of Knossos.

Far more impressive to Alayne's mind were the ornate gold-sheathed doors through which Leucoperses would presently enter . . .

As the seven girls danced, weaving back and forth, the flounces of their dresses rustling and fluttering, Alayne again had to fight against the idea that she was in fact a different being from before, and the most striking thing about the experience was that she seemed quite immune from fear or fatigue.

She glanced at the rapt faces of the other girls, then suddenly understood how it was that year after year the bull-maidens went cheerfully to their deaths and thought themselves so honoured that they wouldn't have changed places with any other girl on earth.

Then, just as she was perilously close to accepting whatever lay in store for her, she caught sight of something out of the corner of her eye that pulled her up short and reminded her that she was a Pendragon's daughter to whom Knossos meant less than nought.

A herald had appeared behind the tiers of seats and was talking urgently to one of the High Priests, who was looking both incredulous and frightened.

Thara had noticed the herald, too. As she danced past Alayne, she muttered : " Something's happened . . ." and then, very faintly, as if from a great distance away Alayne heard three short blasts on a whistle. The invasion was on !

The drums were rolling and the dancers started to retire towards the Snake Goddess's vestibule to prepare for the terrible phase that lay ahead.

Alayne was the last out of the arena, and just before the doors closed, she glimpsed the herald making his way towards the Court officials sitting in the Royal recess, and as whispers of something untoward afoot spread among the assembled priests and priestesses they swayed to and fro like a field of wheat caught by a sudden breeze.

Then the doors closed, and the full-throated singing of the choir drowned the whispers of the priests . . .

In the vestibule Alayne bathed her hands and face in rose-water and found herself next to Thara, but could not speak to her since Greek was the only language they had in common and that was intelligible to everyone else. Instead, they exchanged smiles, and now the spell of Knossos was finally broken and

Alayne could see the whole of the bull cult as ridiculous as it would have seemed to her when she was at home in Dort.

Assisted by the priestesses the girls exchanged their skirts for white breeches, for ahead lay the bull-leaping and all the athletic part of the dance.

Then came the ritual of the last purification. Alayne went through the motions without being really aware of what she was doing, and all the time her mind was searching frantically for a means of escape.

Again she heard a series of whistle blasts, and this time they sounded so near that she half-expected a squad of rescuers to burst into the vestibule, but nothing of the sort happened and the ritual proceeded without interruption up to the point where the leading priestess produced a snake longer than a man's arm, held it above the brazier and intoned prayers to it in a strange and unknown language.

The priestesses chanted a sonorous response to the prayer, the phrase was taken up by the male choir in the arena, and their voices blended with the steady roll of drums which, when it reached its climax, was punctuated by a note on the gong as loud as thunder.

The doors started to open, and now Alayne knew that her one chance of survival lay in prolonging the dance until such time as the invaders and rebels found their way to the arena.

Unfortunately, hours might pass before they arrived, for the location of the arena was a closely guarded secret, known only to high-ranking court officials and priests.

A cymbal crashed and once more she ran into the arena with three dancers on either side of her, and all seven made the squares of scarlet cloth leap and turn like flame above their heads.

The priests had recovered from their agitation. All eyes were watching the dancers intently. There was no sign of the herald, and it was as if the whole assembly had resolved to ignore the happenings beyond the Palace walls.

From the Court's point of view, nothing could be of greater importance than the dance, and if all parties to it played their roles with skill and courage, then Knossos was safe, come the world in arms against it, while a blundering performance and a cowardly bull would presage disaster more surely than any defeat in battle.

Alayne advanced to a point a little beyond the golden post, and came to a standstill as the music stopped. Forming a shallow crescent, the seven girls faced the great gates that would presently admit the bull, and silence filled the arena like an invisible fog as the concourse awaited King Minos's summons to the bull.

The golden trumpet on which the summons would be sounded was carried to the King by the Snake Goddess's arch-priest, and Alayne had a particular reason for keeping her eyes upon the King as he took the trumpet and placed it to his lips, because she wanted to give the lie to something she had been told — that anyone watching the King at that solemn moment would be struck blind by the awful beauty of it.

As it happened, all that Alayne saw was a mild-looking man blowing a trumpet that was far more gorgeous and impressive than himself, and all she heard was a thin, wavering note that died almost as soon as it began, and she was certainly not blinded by the sight. In fact, she could see as well as ever, and now she saw the great gates tremble as the bolts were withdrawn.

She heard Daphne, on her right, catch her breath and then, as music burst through the silence, all the girls flung their scarlet squares across their left shoulders and lunged towards the slowly-opening gates.

Now, in the eyes of the priests, every moment had significance, and weighty considerations depended upon the manner of the bull's entry — whether he came in slowly or at speed, whether he veered to the left, to the right, or, best sign of all, headed for the centre.

Naturally, Alayne was no expert in reading the signs, but she didn't have to be an expert to know that so far all the omens were bad. First there had been the uncertain note blown by the King on the trumpet, and now, although the gates were fully opened, Leucoperses displayed no eagerness to enter the arena. Dimly he could be seen in the shadows beyond the gates where grooms were struggling with him, dragging at his head harness and pricking him with goads in their attempts to make him move.

At last he gave a low bellow, and came trotting into the arena with no more sense of drama than if it had been a meadow. Then he paused, gazing mildly at the seven dancers, and Alayne told the girls to hold their ground.

" The priests will want to know which way he means to go," she said in a stage whisper, " and so far he hasn't shown much preference for any."

The most that could be said was that he looked magnificent. His coat had been washed until it was as white as snow, his trappings were of purple, black and gold, and there was so much gilt on his horns and hoofs that it was hard to believe that they weren't of solid gold.

A cymbal crash startled him, he lowered his head a little, then swung to the left — another bad omen — and Alayne called the appropriate figure of the dance.

The girl nearest Leucoperses brought him into position by using her cloth, then made a neat, but unspectacular leap across his shoulders, and was caught well enough by Thara.

Puzzled, the great bull turned in his tracks and came ambling down the centre of the arena. Alayne saw her chance to do a nimble, and quite safe double leap-frog — Daphne was there to catch her — and moved quickly to face the bull. He scented her, and then an extraordinary change came over him. He lowered his head, every muscle in his body grew taut, and when Alayne looked at his eyes expecting to see anger, she saw nothing except the most abject terror. The bull was backing away from her. And then Alayne knew that he remembered her as some horrifying creature that had once blinded him, destroying his power of action.

She stepped towards him, flourishing her scarlet cloth, and with a bellow of anguish that momentarily drowned the music, he wheeled frantically away from her, scattering the girls, and plunged madly towards the gates with all the force his great body could muster.

Dust rose from the arena in clouds, and then the bull hit the gates with a crash that must have been heard throughout Knossos.

Thara screamed : " The gates are down ! "

That was enough for Alayne. Making sure that Thara was with her, she raced for the gates — one of which hung drunkenly from its hinges while the other was flat on the ground — and leapt over the body of a groom knocked down by the terror-stricken bull.

The corridors seemed dark after the arena's brilliance. Men were scurrying hither and thither but none tried to stop the two girls — they were goddesses now, immortal and immensely powerful.

They had no idea of their whereabouts. They only knew that

they were below ground, so, whenever they came upon flights of stairs leading upwards, they ascended them, and soon they found themselves in a part of the Palace far more gorgeously appointed than their own quarters.

Passages led into other passages, rooms into other rooms. This part of the Palace was utterly deserted, and faintly the sounds of battle were borne to them, the shouting and the war-cries, the whistle of the arrows and the crash of bronze against bronze.

" I think we're lost," whispered Alayne, " but we must have reached ground-level by now."

Cautiously she opened a door, and they found themselves in a sumptuously-furnished bedroom as large as the whole of the bull-maidens' suite. Scent hung in the air, beautiful dresses were strewn on the bed, and the room evidently belonged to some great lady — perhaps to the Queen herself.

Alayne tiptoed to one of the windows and peered out between its slats.

" We're above ground-level !" she exclaimed. " We're at least one floor up, if not two."

She opened the window, and then they could see that parts of Knossos were in flames and the great smoke-clouds rolled over the city. The noise was tremendous, and now it seemed that the battle raged immediately below the Palace walls. They were looking down into one of the courtyards, and the only people in sight were the guards manning the gate, and the archers lining its battlements.

The gate was being attacked with a battering-ram, and every blow seemed to shake the Palace to its foundations.

" We clearly can't get out of the Palace," began Alayne, then broke off as they heard the sound of men hurrying along the passage outside. She raced to the door, slammed it in the face of a man who was just about to come in, then bolted it.

" A temple soldier," she whispered to Thara. " They're searching for us."

The man hammered on the door, ordering them to open in the name of the arch-priest, and he was quickly joined by others.

" We're bull-maidens ! " shouted Alayne. " You daren't touch us and you know it."

The men, acting under the arch-priest's protection, were not to be intimidated, and already the door was starting to crack as they threw themselves against it. The girls barricaded it with furniture, even dragging the great bed across the room, until Alayne heard something that sent her hurrying to the window — the war-cry of Sarm !

The battering-ram had done its work, and now a battle was raging in the courtyard. The Palace guards were falling back before the onslaught of the invaders, and Alayne recognised Gervor of Sarm in the thick of the fight, as well as two warriors from Dort.

She shouted to them, but couldn't make herself heard above the noise, and then she ran back to the door which was still holding out against the temple soldiers.

" You fools ! " she shouted to them. " The invaders are over-running the Palace. If you hurry you've still got time to get out through the Labyrinth."

It was a shot in the dark, but it appeared to work. The thudding against the door suddenly ceased, and she heard the men muttering amongst themselves. Her suggestion must have made sense to them, and a few moments later she heard them running back along the passage.

She joined Thara at the window, and found that the battle in the courtyard was virtually over. Now fighting was going on within the building, and the two girls gazed at each other, undecided what course to take.

" If we leave now," said Alayne at length, " we'll probably walk straight into the guards, and they'll kill us."

" You mean they'll blame us for their defeat ? "

" Yes. I think we'd better stay where we are, in the hope of getting away after dark."

An urgent hammering on the door interrupted her, and a voice shouted : " Open up ! '

" An invader ? " whispered Thara, and Alayne shook her head.

" No, a guard, going by his Greek."

" I can hear you talking ! " shouted the man. " Open up ! " He added : " Is that the bull-maidens' suite ? "

That wasn't a question a guard would ask, and intrigued, Alayne decided to break her silence.

" What do you want with the bull-maidens ? " she asked.

" To rescue them ! "

" He could be a rebel," whispered Thara. " Ask him for the password."

Alayne did so, and the man's reply set her fears at rest. " The Lion Roars ! " he cried, and the girls started dragging the furniture away from the door as fast as they could move it.

Thara unbolted the door, and as it opened Alayne almost fainted with astonishment. Facing her was Orontes, the shipmaster, and with him, as well as three or four warriors, was her cousin, Artor of Sarm.

She embraced him, and for nearly a minute was too moved to speak. Artor was almost as incoherent, but at last managed to say : " We'd given you up for dead, Alayne. Our first prisoners told us that we were a day late in our timing, and then, when you didn't turn up at the Pharos . . . "

A sudden burst of cheering reached them from another part of the Palace, and a few moments later a warrior appeared to tell them that the guard had surrendered.

The great adventure was over. King Minos had been put to flight, and never again would the youths and maidens of other lands have to die that mighty Knossos might live . . .

THE END